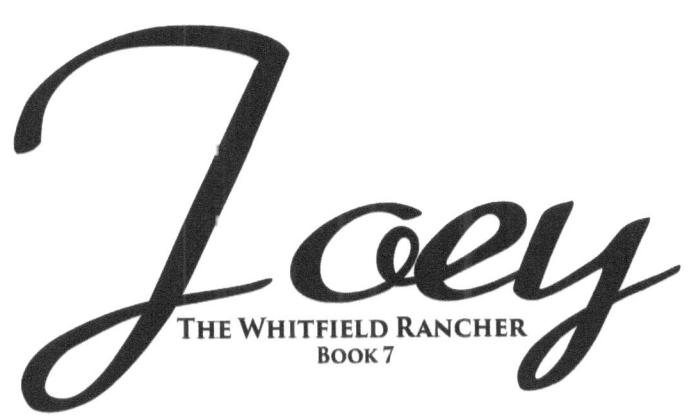

THE WHITFIELD RANCHER
BOOK 7

KATHI S. BARTON

This is a work of fiction. Names, characters, places, and incidents are products of the author's imagination or are used fictitiously and are not to be construed as real. Any resemblance to actual events, locations, organizations, or persons, living or dead, is entirely coincidental.

World Castle Publishing, LLC
Pensacola, Florida
Copyright © Kathi S. Barton 2021
Paperback ISBN: 9781953271662
eBook ISBN: 9781953271679
First Edition World Castle Publishing, LLC, January 25, 2021
http://www.worldcastlepublishing.com
Licensing Notes
Cover: Karen Fuller
Editor: Maxine Bringenberg

Prologue

"Autumn Hunter?" Autumn stood up and made her way to the medical assistant. "Your name is really Autumn? Your parents hate you or something?"

The same question, along with a few others she got every time she met someone new. Smiling, she did not tell the assistant they did indeed hate her, but not until later, after she'd been older. Instead, she stepped up on the scale and thought about how much weight she'd lost in the last year and a half. Being terrified of being caught up in shit and on the run all the time would do that, she supposed.

"You're here about your belly issues and the results of the test, correct?" Autumn told her she was also out of her pain medication, could she get a refill. "We'll have to clear it through the doctor first. Once he's told you—"

The assistant looked at the folder in her hand, then at Autumn. She knew it was bad, but how bad was something she was about to learn. Reaching over to take the folder from her, Autumn read the words there before the woman asked for it back. Handing it to her, Autumn was at a loss for words.

"He'll be able to explain your options." It was on the tip of her tongue to tell her she knew what her options were. There was only one. Death. It was just how she chose to do it. "You'll need those pills. I'll make sure you have samples before you leave."

Nodding, Autumn wondered if she should even stay. They'd told her— Well, she'd found out she had stomach cancer. She supposed knowing how she got it would be good, but it wouldn't change the outcome. Standing up, Autumn was ready to leave when the doctor came into the room.

"I'm sorry, Miss Hunter." She nodded, sure that he knew she'd read the notes on her chart. "There are things we can do to make things easier on you. A great many more than we had even ten years ago. We'll make you as—"

"How long do I have? I mean, you know that, don't you?" He nodded. "I don't know if you remember my first visit with you, but I don't care for bullshit answers. Just tell me how long I have and whatever pertinent information I need right now. The rest of whatever you tell me is going to go in one ear and out the other otherwise."

"Yes, I remember. You have just about a month.

I don't know how far you got to read, but it's spread all through your body. Had someone bothered to give you good care when you were ill the first time, you would have had better chances of survival than you do now, two years later." She asked him what he thought caused it. "Someone tried to poison you, as you know. And that weakened your immune system, which was ripe ground for cancer to dig in. I'm really sorry, Autumn."

"I need to go." He nodded and told her to come back in a week. "Do you think I'll be around then?"

"I hope so. You're going to hurt a good deal more than you are now. I'll make sure you have what you need to deal with it. Autumn, whoever did this to you, it's the same as if they'd used a gun to kill you. In fact, as you like it right to the truth, a bullet would have been much faster and far less painful for you."

"I know, but there is nothing I can do about that now." Autumn got off the table and started to pull on her jacket. "I don't know what I'm going to do right now, so I'll call you soon and set something up."

"Autumn, please don't end your life." She looked at him and realized he had every right to think that would be something she'd do. "I promise you, when the time comes, you'll not feel a thing. I'll be there with you to make sure of it."

"I promised someone once that I'd not do that. And even though she's gone, I won't break my promise to her." She could feel the tears building up in her eyes.

"I need to go and think. Your assistant said she had some samples I could have, maybe."

The woman came in and handed her a white bag. It was heavy, but Autumn didn't bother looking inside. She had enough to think about instead of whether or not she had been given a bag of rocks.

Once out in the sunshine — the rain had stopped for now — she pulled on her sunglasses and made her way to her car. Crying without anyone seeing was an easy way to avoid the strange looks that she got.

Getting inside her car, she drove to her home. There had been a plan to pick up a few things at the grocery store, but Autumn didn't feel like that now. As she pulled into the driveway, she saw a car there that she recognized and decided she wasn't in the mood for her sister either. Moving up to the porch, she saw April sitting there with an angry look on her face.

"You locked the door. And my key doesn't work anymore." Pulling out her keys, Autumn unlocked the door and slipped them in her pocket rather than her purse. "Why would you change the locks? I've been coming and going out of this house since before you were born."

"Only because someone carried you in and out. You're only eighteen months older than me. I changed the locks because it's my house now, and not everyone's *drop in whenever you're in town* place. What do you want, April? I've had a shitty day, and you're not going to make it any better."

"Well, aren't you in a shitty mood?" She didn't point out that she'd just told her that. When April opened the refrigerator door, Autumn pushed her own body against it and shut the door. "I want some juice. You always have the best kind."

"I have the best kind because I like the best kind. I don't care for sharing it today. What. Do. You. Want?" April sat down. Flopped would have been a better word for it, she supposed. "This is getting you no closer to leaving me alone. I want to think."

"Grant is kicking me out of the house." Autumn asked her why she thought she'd care. "I know you never liked him, but he was my husband. We have a child together."

"First of all, I like Grant. It's you I don't care for. And it's debatable if the child is his or not. I told you he wasn't as stupid as you seemed to hope he was. For Christ's sake, April, the man is a doctor. It's doubtful to me that they allow you to practice medicine when you're stupid." April asked her why she was taking his side in this. "Because, and this should be no surprise to you, you're a bitch. You cheated on him several times in his own bed. The kid you shove aside for some other rabble isn't his, and he's a nice man. I said, I like him."

"Uncle Ross should never have left you this house. There are seven of us girls from his sister, and it should have been divided between all of us and not just you."

Autumn explained to her, yet again, that he didn't like her either. "You're very obtuse today. What's up with you?"

"I have cancer from the poison Mom and Dad gave me, and it's spread throughout my body." April just stared at her for a moment, then asked her who she was leaving the house to. "Get out, April. Now, before I hurt you. You're wondering why Grant kicked you to the curb? Perhaps you should record yourself having a conversation with someone and listen to it. Maybe that will give you a clue. You certainly don't have any compassion anywhere in you. And the word you meant to use isn't obtuse. It's fucking rude. Get your insults correct. Get out and don't come back. Ever."

Shoving her sister out the door, she locked it after checking to make sure she had the keys. Then she bolted the door, going to the back and side doors to do the same. If anyone came around now and thought to get in, she was going to blow them away with her uncle's shotgun in the cupboard.

"He left me the house because I stayed with him for four years while the rest of you acted like he was nothing more than a bank account for yourself." She was glad he'd pulled his money from the bank after having a wall safe put in the house. There were no credit cards for them to steal. No checks to write out for cash. And everything he owned had been changed to her as the owner with him so no one could take whatever they wished from a dying old man.

The house wasn't much—two bedrooms, a living room, kitchen, and a single bathroom. What it did have going for it was the three hundred acres surrounding it, as well as the rigging that pumped out oil, the wide creek that supplied water to several towns below it, as well as a mine. The mine alone produced coal and gems, such as gold and diamonds, at a nice rate. No one, just her and Uncle Ross's attorney, knew the amount of land she'd been left, nor the other operations supplying her with a good amount of income yearly.

Autumn sat down on the couch and thought about her day. She had had so much planned for the afternoon after her appointment, but all that had gone to shit. Knowing you didn't have long to live sure put a damper on things, she thought.

The seven of them that April had been talking about were her sisters, all but one older than her—April was the closest to her in age—and all named for a month in the year. Autumn had always wondered if they'd planned to have twelve children.

The sisters were named January, February, and April. There was May, June, and July, September, and then her, Autumn. The reason she was the odd one out was because she'd been born in September too—the thirtieth, as a matter of fact. Her name would have been October had she been born just twelve hours later. That was only one of the reasons her parents had hated her.

Autumn was also the seventh child of a seventh son. It might not have made a lick of difference that she'd been born in September if she'd been a boy, what they'd been told they were to have. But being a daughter, the seventh one, it caused all kinds of shit to happen. Her father had a long line of sevenths born to his side of the family. It would only be skipped over when there was a different sex born to that line as the seventh child, such as her being a boy. Autumn was the seventh of a long line of seventh same sex children. Autumn was magical.

"But not magical enough to keep from getting cancer." Trying not to think about what her parents had done to her so they could, she supposed, cut off her magic, she looked at the things from her mailbox.

Credit offers were nothing new to her, and she made sure they were shredded. With those applications in the wrong hands, her sisters would cause a disaster. She had a cell phone bill, as well as a bill for something called Dispatchers. Opening it up, she knew just who had put her name on the billing. It was really too bad on January's part. Autumn had made it perfectly clear that any bills not okayed in writing by her would not be paid. She would have thought all her sisters would have figured this out by now.

Pulling out her phone and making the call come from a restricted number, she didn't think January would answer. When she did, Autumn asked her about Dispatchers.

"Oh, they're this amazing company that will pick up anything you order from anywhere in the state and bring it to you within twenty-four hours. That way, with me just having a baby, I don't have to bundle her up and take her out. It's so she won't get sick." Autumn pointed out that it was eighty-five degrees where she lived. "I know that, silly. But she could still get germs. Why do you ask?"

"I'm not paying this bill. Not one dime of it, January. I made that clear to you guys when Uncle Ross died." January tried telling her about germs and the baby. "Since I didn't knock you up, nor did I have her for you, she is not my responsibility. Not now, not ever."

"You got the house, Autumn. The least you can do is pay for a few things extra for the rest of us. What's it going to take for you to realize you're not all that special?" Autumn thought about her sister's house and tossed an expensive glass vase to the floor. "Did you do that? Damn it, Autumn, that was a wedding present from his parents. You'll pay for that."

"Yeah, good luck on trying to prove I did it from Ohio when you live in California. I'm not paying this bill. And I have no idea how many things you've had delivered, but for six grand, I would have thought it would have been cheaper to let the baby have a cold instead of paying this bill." January called her a bitch. "Perhaps, but you'll be hearing from my attorney."

Hanging up on her felt wonderful. When the

phone rang again, her sister's number, she turned the phone off and put it back in the coffee table drawer. It was only used to call them anyway. Feeling better about herself and what had happened, Autumn decided to have a salad for dinner.

~~~

"It's been two years. How do you feel now?" Joey told Tanner he felt like he could hold his own with his magic now. "Good. I'm sorry to spring this on you, but you don't have a lot of time to get to your mate. She's having issues."

"What sort of issues?" When Tanner didn't tell him, it left him to guess or rape his mind again. "Tell me, Tanner, so I can tell if I really do need to hurry along to get to her."

"She's dying. And soon, from what I've found out." Joey asked him what she was dying from. "I don't have all the details just yet, but some form of cancer. She'll need you to heal her before the big guns, as Ollie used to say, come for her."

"How long will it take us to get to her?" Tanner pointed to the tiny looking house that sat back from the road a good way. "We've been here the entire time?"

"Yes. I didn't know she was so bad when we came here. But I thought it could do us no harm by being as close as we could in the event she needed you. I should have told you, I suppose, but I don't like having things changed around when I have no say over them." Joey just cocked a brow at him. "Saving you from the flames is not the same thing. We needed to make sure of your abilities, and in the end, we were so wrong about that."

"Yes, no shit."

Joey had been sleeping in his tent for the entire time they'd been here. With the magic he had, he'd been warm and toasty when the cold came in. Now it was summer again, and he was starting to feel the heat at night. He also wanted a meal he didn't cook over the grill and a long hot shower.

As he packed up his gear, he realized Tanner was gone again. It was just as well. They had worked hard in the two years, and he wanted to move on as well. Gathering up his gear, he started toward the house. Might as well get this over with. Meeting his mate might be good or bad, but he'd not know until he got there.

The screaming had him dropping everything he had and taking off at a run. His tiger took him over before they got too far, and the screaming was cut off. Whatever was going on, he knew it was pain and not just someone letting off some steam.

Chapter 1

Autumn watched the man pace back and forth. He did it very well as if he'd made a job of it, and now he was going for some sort of medal. When he stopped to look at her, she decided she'd had enough of him being there and sat up. Sitting there for several seconds, she realized how easy that had been.

"I'm not as weak as I was an hour ago." He sat down on the floor in front of her. "You have some explaining to do, I think. First of all, who are you?"

"Joey Whitfield. You're Autumn Hunter." She nodded. "You're feeling better because I'm your mate. Also, I do believe you've been getting a little help from a vampire friend of mine, Tanner. I can smell him in this room, as well as on you. Do you have any more questions for me right now?"

"Yes. You chased off my sister. Not that I'm upset about that, but how did you know she was here? I'm assuming you were lurking around outside and saw her trying to kill me." He told her he was miles away. "I see. Actually, I don't. Why are you sure—? Never mind. I was going to ask you how you were so sure you're my mate when I realized I'm feeling better. You're not just a cat, a tiger, are you?"

"No." She thought he'd say more, but he smiled at her instead. "You should know a few things before I explain what I am. First of all, you still have cancer. I could have taken it away from you, but I won't do anything to you that I don't ask about first. I can understand you'd want it gone—it's a nasty thing to have. But I want you to trust me, and just doing things to you won't have us starting out on a good note."

"I don't want it in me. However, you should know I got it because of my parents. They hated me. I'm not sure why...well, I know a little. I'm the seventh child of a seventh child." He nodded. "How do you know that?"

"You're magical. I'm assuming you didn't want to share what you had with your family, and that made you a target." She nodded. "I don't believe you to be selfish, as they do, but smart. Using the magic you have would have drained you to be nothing more than a shell of what you were. Not giving into them saved you to become my mate. Thank you."

"They poisoned me—my parents. I believe my sisters were in on it as well. But as it was years ago, I don't have any proof." Joey put out his hand, and a ball—a sphere, she figured it would be called — appeared. As it grew in size, she watched it as she finished telling him what she'd later found out. "It weakened my immune system, which made it a prime place for cancer to dig in and take over. What is that?"

"Magic. It's what I can help you with. But, and this is very important, I want you to know that by taking this from me, you'll bond us in a way that we'll be true mates. You'll also get magic. How much or what it will be, I have no idea. But you'll get it." She didn't reach for it, even though it had left his hand and floated in the air in front of her. Autumn asked Joey what he was again. "Magical. I don't know that there is a name for what I can do or what I am. I nearly died when I was in my twenties, and a vampire and Aurora, the queen of faeries, saved me. In doing so, mixed with the magic I received from being with a family of tigers and my age, I'm an oddity to even them."

"You're older than you look." He nodded. "You don't talk much, do you? I mean, you will if just to answer a question, but you don't really converse much."

"I've been a loner for most of my life. Even as a child, I stayed away from people. It kept me safer. I lived in an abusive home when I was a kid. The Whitfields adopted me and gave me a good and supportive home. However, the damage had been done, and I didn't cope well with not just people, but all things." The orb seemed to vibrate. "The police are on their way here. Your sister has told them you have a lion in the house, and you told it to attack her for no reason. Does she know the difference between a lion and a tiger?"

"She probably doesn't care. It's all about her." Joey looked at the opening that used to house a door. "That's going to be a dead giveaway that something happened here. We'll have to come up with a story, or we might have some explaining to do that I don't know enough about right now to give a good fib."

He stood up. The orb stayed near her but seemed to turn toward Joey. When Joey put his hands on either side of the opening, a door appeared. Not the same one that had been there before, but one she'd been wanting since her uncle Ross had passed away.

Tossing the covers off her, she decided she wanted a shower. Not just a quick washup, but a full shower with nice soaps and shampoo. Standing had her sway a little, but Joey made sure she didn't fall, and she looked up at him. He had the most beautiful blue eyes she'd ever seen.

"I don't know what to do now." He said he didn't either. "I'm going to take a shower, and when I get back out, you and I will talk. If the police arrive before I get back, you can deal with them, can't you?"

Nodding, he let her go, and she moved toward the bathroom. Joey told her to be careful, as she was still weak. As she was moving by the couch she'd been sleeping on for the past couple of months, she realized how bad the room looked. Tissues were everywhere.

There were empty glasses as well as other things she didn't want to think very hard on. Thinking it would be nice to have a nice spruced up house, she saw the dust move off the little end table that was cluttered with remotes and books and was glad Joey was doing this. Perhaps she'd help out when she got back.

The shower was heavenly. Not only did she wash her hair four times simply because she could, but she also scrubbed her body harder than she had in a while. The little sit down baths she'd been able to give herself were all right, but this was satisfying in a way she'd not felt in a long time.

Now she had the task of figuring out something to wear. Nothing would fit, she was sure of that. It had been a long time since she'd worn anything other than slip on pants and T-shirts. Thinking of how wonderful it would feel to have on a pair of nice jeans and a pretty blouse, she had to sit down on the edge of her bed when the same thing she'd had in mind appeared on her body. The orb moved to be in front of her face again.

"You really want me to touch you, don't you?" The thing nodded at her. "Will it hurt? I don't know why I think you'd not lie to me any more than Joey would, but I'm sick of being in constant pain."

It shook its head, and she could have sworn it smiled at her. It moved closer to her, nearly touching her nose. Lifting her hand up to touch the blue orb, the warmth coming from it felt like she was sitting out in the sun sunbathing. Autumn wrapped both hands around it and pulled it to her body.

Autumn woke lying in her bed. It was dark out, so she knew she'd been down for a while. It hadn't hurt, that was true, but it had made her feel like she'd been rejuvenated several times over. Stretching, she nearly screamed when she felt movement beside her. Turning slowly, she looked into the eyes of Joey.

"The couch isn't long enough for me. I didn't mean to be here when you woke." She nodded. "You've been asleep for four days now. I was beginning to worry you weren't going to wake anytime soon."

"Four days?" He nodded. "The last thing I remember was the orb. It said it would not hurt me. But I guess it did knock me out for a bit."

"You've been sleeping. And healing. There are things I must tell you that I'm sure the doctor who was caring for you didn't. You had cancer on your brain, as well as throughout your blood stream. In a few more days, had I not come here, you would have been dead. I'm sorry." She asked him why he was sorry. "That I didn't come sooner. I didn't insist you let me heal you. I could have lost you."

"But I'm all right now." He said she was perfect. "My sister. She sent the police here. I guess you must have handled that as well."

"Yes." He smiled at her. "I don't believe she'll be coming around here anytime soon, but she'll return. I think some of them are unbalanced in their scheming to get something from you. They think since you have magic, you should give up the house to them. A couple of them do, anyway. They don't know about the gem farm or the diamonds, do they?"

"I'm not going to ask you how you found out." He said that was probably good, but it wasn't bad. "Did the others come by while I was sleeping? I'm assuming since you said they weren't right in the head, you've met them."

"No, but you have. If you were to search your mind, you'd find some of my memories in with yours. I have your memories of you growing up. You had a terrible childhood—I'm sorry for that." She did search her mind for memories of his and shied away from them. Horrific memories weren't anything she wanted to see right now. Joey spoke again. "Although she and the others are pretty stupid. Did you know they've got a restraining order against you? That makes no sense whatsoever."

"Once you see them all face to face, you're going to realize that is the least of their issues. I'm suddenly starving." He said he could cook for her. "All right. And even though I've only slept, I feel like I need another shower. Would you mind if I did?"

"No. You enjoy it. I'll make us some steaks and baked potatoes. How about a chocolate cake too?" He was moving out of the room as he spoke, and she didn't bother telling him there weren't any potatoes in the house, much less the ingredients for a chocolate anything.

This time when she entered her tiny bathroom, she thought of herself naked and was glad to see it worked both ways. Autumn didn't linger in her shower like she had the first time. She was starving, for one thing, and she felt too energized to just be idle. Getting dressed again, she wanted to try on different things, but once again, her belly said it needed to be filled. Going out of the bedroom, she looked around the living room and stood stock still.

"This is lovely." Joey came out of the kitchen with an apron on that she knew she didn't own, as well as a spatula in his hand. There was, if she wasn't mistaken, frosting—chocolate—on the end of it. "Did you do this?"

"No. How do you like your steak?" When she told him rare, she wondered at that too. Normally she didn't care for red meat. Not that she couldn't eat it, but it wasn't on her list of go to meats. "Are you implying I did this? I was sleeping, if you remember."

"I do. Come on. Dinner is ready." She was going to have to hurt him if he didn't get with it and say more. When he stopped in the room, holding the platter with the steaks he'd just brought in from the outside, Autumn felt herself tense up as well. "One of your sisters is coming up the driveway. Her anger is palpable. She is thinking that if you don't die soon, she's going to fix that for you. She seems to think you're leaving everything you were left by your uncle to her. I don't know which one it is, as I've never met her."

"Probably July." She asked him if he'd let her eat now. "I don't know how she's going to like me being well, but that's her problem. I'm starving."

He put a steak on her plate, then one on his. There was already a potato as large as her head on the thing. Also, he'd made tea. The kitchen smelled of chocolate and cream. The steak was as tender as anything she'd ever cut into before. Putting the first bite in her mouth, she moaned, then frowned when someone knocked on the front door.

"Tell her to go away." Joey got up when the doorbell sounded as if she was laying on it. "I'm feeling good, and I don't want her to fuck that up for me. I don't know why they give a shit about this house. It's not like anything they live in and pay a mortgage on."

July followed Joey into the kitchen. Deciding she was hungrier than she was upset, between bites, Autumn asked her what she wanted. July told Joey she wanted hers cooked well done and handed him the plate from the table. Joey just pushed another chair, which again, she didn't have, to the table and sat down with her.

"Aren't you just a rude bastard? That's my dinner. Coming out here, I had to leave before I got to eat. The very least you can do is feed me." She reached for Joey's dinner, and he growled at her. "What is wrong with you?"

"I'm hungry as well. This is our dinner. Since you came here uninvited, then you'll have to do without." Joey got up to get a refill on their drinks and didn't offer one to July.

"April was here the other day and said you threatened to have her arrested for trespassing. That wasn't nice of you, Autumn. We're family. She also said you were on your death bed. What are you doing up and around eating steaks with your nurse? You do know you're not to eat with the help, right?"

"What he is to me in none of your business. I will tell you, however, that you might well be arrested too if you don't get out of here now, July. I'm having too good of a time, and you're fucking with it." She looked at Joey. "This is amazing. I don't think I've had a grilled out steak in forever. Thank you for this."

"My pleasure." He finished off his meal before she did. When he got up, the chair he'd been sitting in disappeared. If July noticed, she didn't comment. "We'll have cake and ice cream later."

"Hello? I'm sitting right here." Autumn looked at her sister. "What the hell are you trying to prove here, Autumn? That you're no longer sick? It won't work. I've spoken to your doctor, and he said he gave you only a month to live several days ago. Why you are still up and around is beyond me. Also, I do hope you know that, even if you didn't make out a will, I'll be getting this house and the land. I need the money."

"I'm not sick. I don't have cancer anymore, and for the first time in a long while, I feel like I can kick your ass." Autumn stood up and stood over her sister. "You have five minutes to be off my property, July. If you're not, not only am I going to press charges against you for trespassing, but I'm going to tell the police you broke into my home. Where did you get that key anyway?"

"I had it made." She looked at Joey, then back at her sister. "All I needed to do was tell the man who you had change the locks that you were ill, which he knew, and that you weren't answering your phone. Which he'd tried to call you as well. Don't change them again, Autumn, or so help me, I'll come back here with an axe. Why don't you just fucking die?"

"I'm not going to now." She didn't know why she didn't explain more to her sister, but she thought that was the right way to go. "Get out. And don't return."

When July left her, she turned to look at Joey. He didn't move from leaning against the counter, but he was smiling at her. Asking him what he thought was so funny, instead of answering her, he moved towards her.

"I have family members in very high places. I was just talking to my mom and Aunt Dylan, and they're looking into why your sisters are so hard up to get this house from you. They, your sisters, know nothing of the gems or the other things you're having done here, do they?" She said she'd not told them anything. "According to Aunt Dylan, that's the only thing that has kept you alive this long."

"I have money." He said he did as well. "Wait. Whitfield. You said you had friends in high places. Your father, he's the president that has done so well for this country."

"My uncle." All sorts of things she'd seen about his family in the paper popped into her head then. "They want to meet you. All of them. But as you and I both are somewhat loners, they're willing to meet you a little at a time."

"Can you take them all at once?" He said he could if he had to. "No then. I only want to meet them how you'd do it. I'm not usually so alone, Joey. I used to be pretty out there when I was around others. What if this is a mistake? That the two of us aren't mates at all?"

"We are." He moved by her and to the front door. "My parents. I didn't invite them, but they're here. Are you all right with that?"

Was she? She didn't know for sure. But nodding at him, he opened the front door and was engulfed into the arms of two people. These, Autumn thought, were what parents should be like.

~~~

Shadow loved the young woman. She was very careful to include Joey in all her decision making. Autumn had already agreed, with Joey's input, that they'd need a better home. And bigger. Even as they talked about what she and Joey would need in a bigger home, Autumn seemed worried about all the money it was going to take to build it.

"Look at me, Autumn." She looked at the beautiful woman, who seemed to want to turn away as if Shadow's confidence made her nervous. "I want you to remember two things about me. All right? First of all, I will never harm you. None of us will. You're as much a part of our family now as Joey is. Second thing, you're as confident as I am. Perhaps even more so. Joey and you, you're suited in ways you cannot imagine right now."

"He's very quiet." Shadow told her he'd always been. "He told me that. Joey also said he's not good around lots of people. I thrive for that. At least I did before I got sick. I'm not sure what he sees in me."

"More than likely the same thing all of us see when we look at you—a beautiful, confident woman who has more brains than anyone has given you credit for. Also, you have a lot of street smarts, something I'm sure saved you more often than your education has. Joey has a good mate in you. Someone that will more than likely bring him back to us." She asked her why he was so standoffish. Autumn looked at Joey, and Shadow could see the love she had for her little boy, a man now. "It's his story to tell, I'm afraid. Most of it, I'm sure, even I'm not aware of. His only confidant, the man he trusted with more secrets than he did us, passed away before he left us this last time—his Grandpa Ollie."

"He loved Ollie because he never judged him.

Never spoke to him in a loud voice or with meanness. Memories of the older man came into my mind just now. Their talks. The two of them with their heads together while fishing. The times Grandpa Ollie picked Joey up and shook him hard to get him back on track." Shadow looked at Autumn when Joey and his father went into the yard. "I know he's not your blood son, but he looks like you. I'm sure people told you that." She said they had, and smiled. "He told me he's magical. I don't know why I know this, but you have no idea of the events that kept him alive the night of the robbery, do you?"

"Only that he had to be saved. I have a feeling Tanner had a great deal to do with him still being alive." She told her about the faerie queen, Aurora. "That explains a great deal. She would have made him powerful all on her own. You have magic as well. Not from Joey."

"Yes. Not nearly as much as I have now, but I was the seventh child of a seventh child. Also, few know this, but I was the seventh generation to be born the seventh of seven." Shadow asked if she could bring someone here that would be able to help her with her magic. "I thought you would help me."

"No, I'm sorry. I wish I could. But the only people that can help you are the ones that gave Joey what he has now. He's more powerful now than when he left us. To find you, I guess." Shadow smiled. "Aurora will drop in, but she wanted me to warn you that she's a faerie, and she met you before."

The light that entered the living room she and Autumn were sitting in was like the orb, a great ball of magic. Shadow could see the tiny queen inside, and the happiness and warmth there also filled her mind. When Aurora stood in the living room, Autumn smiled, like an old friend had come to visit her.

"You. You saved my life that night." Aurora said she had. That she'd known long ago who she was to Joey. Looking at Shadow, Autumn explained. "It was the night my father tossed me outside in the cold. He did that often enough I began stashing things out there to eat and cover up with. But this time was different. I was chained to the fencing surrounding our property. I had nothing on but a pair of panties and the chains around my neck."

Autumn spoke about that night as if she were living it over again. Shadow was an artist and could paint the picture the younger woman described. Autumn did such a wonderful job of telling her about the back yard, Shadow was sure it was burnt into her memory for all time.

"I don't remember the supposed crime I had committed. It didn't take much for them to take things out on me. Even as I've gotten older, I don't understand why it was me they hated so very much. But once I was out there, chained up, I decided I'd do what they wanted and die." At eight, Autumn knew about suicide and how to commit it. That had to be the saddest thing she'd ever heard, Shadow thought. "I stood up and leaned out against the chains. I didn't fight to breathe. I was going to die by my own hand so I'd not hurt, not suffer anymore. As the lights behind my eyelids began to sparkle, telling me I couldn't breathe, I heard a soft voice speak to me." Autumn looked at Aurora.

"I told you that you were better than them. I was correct, too." Aurora sat down beside Autumn and took her hands into hers. "Over the years, you have proven you are very worthy of saying that to them. That night I warmed you, kept you warm throughout the night and into the morning. Each time you were sent out, a small faerie would tell me, and I'd do it over and over for you. Supplying you with not just a warm body, but food as well as water. You, in turn, did so much for us. Planting the flowers on the other side of the fence for us to use. You picked up trash along pathways. Little things like that have meant so much to us. Even now, you plant flowers and prune back your trees. When you leave the branches for us, the faeries can build homes and furniture. You, along with Joey, have given us so much more than anyone has. Even the Whitfields' help, as much as it means to us, is less than the thoughtfulness of children who have so very little."

"Thank you." Aurora nodded and asked her what her plans were now. "I have no idea. We've really only just met, and I've been dealing with the magic he gave me to heal, as well as having two of my sisters come by and annoy me. Do you suppose they'll ever quit?"

"They will when they are dead." Shadow hadn't meant to sound so positive about that, nor should she have said it so harshly. But Autumn only nodded, as if she figured that would be the only way to stop them.

When Joey and his father came back into the house, she knew something had happened. What it was, she didn't have any idea, but she could tell by the look her son gave Autumn that he was deeply in love with her. Shadow thought the two of them very well suited.

"Hello, Lady Aurora." Joey was hugged by the other woman, tightly and longer than she thought her son was comfortable with. "Did you get my message? I have all the plants you wanted seeds from, all dried and ready to be bagged up. I might have gotten more than you requested, but I'm sure you can use them."

Aurora explained, "There are certain plants in this area that are dying out. I thought if Joey could find them and harvest the seeds, we'd be able to plant them in a better place. The effect they have on this area of land isn't all that big, but there will be less and less of them as the farmers spray for them." Autumn told her she didn't allow anyone to use sprays on her land. "And they don't. I thank you for that as well."

"Joey has decided that if Autumn wants to, he'd like to return home with us. I told him how his grandpa Oliver and grandma have moved in with us, and their home is now his. But he said he'd have to speak to Autumn about it first." At Blake's comment, Shadow wondered if the woman would want to stay here, where her family was. Then she dismissed that, because she'd been doing some research on them and knew they weren't close. "The mines are in good shape and producing gems at a very good rate. Also, the diamond mines hidden well within the coal mines are providing Autumn with a good deal of money."

"I don't have a great deal to do with that. Mostly it's the miners doing the work. And they're being overseen by their foreman, who worked with my uncle before he passed away. It's nothing I have to be here for." Shadow asked if Aurora could send some of her people there to keep an eye on things if they decided to move. She said it would be an honor. "I loved living here when my uncle Ross was alive, but it hasn't ever meant much to me as a home. A place to live, that's all it is to me. If you'd like to move back home to be around your parents and family, Joey, I'm all for that."

"What will you do with this house?" She told Joey she didn't know, and Shadow was never prouder of her son than she was in that minute. He wasn't pushing his mate into anything but letting her decide. Autumn asked Blake what he'd do with it.

"If it were me, I'd remove the house. We could take care of that before we leave. Or you can leave it here as a rental for someone that works in the mines for you." She said her sisters would hurt them. "Then I'd remove it. But only if you're sure, Autumn. Once it's removed, we cannot put it back."

"I understand. You'll be using magic." Blake nodded. "I'm just worried someone will try and build something else here. Or move a home in here, like a trailer of some sort."

"No one will be able to if you don't wish it to happen." Autumn stared at Joey when he spoke. Autumn seemed to understand what he was saying more than Shadow did. When the younger woman nodded, Joey just simply snapped his fingers. "It's done. If you'd like to pack all this up and go through it later, you and I together, we can make that happen as well. It won't take us but a few minutes to clear this house out. Then Dad and I will make sure the house is gone. To the ground."

"Yes, I'd like that."

Almost as if Autumn had said to start, things began to disappear in the house. Standing up, the couch beneath her disappeared, along with several books and a lamp. Standing as still as she could, Shadow wondered where Joey had gotten so much in the way of magic. And Autumn too. Before they left the home to wait on it to be taken down, the place was emptied of every item, and two overnight bags were sitting by the limo they'd arrived in.

"I hope you don't mind that we're going back with you."

Shadow looked where the empty house stood and

back at the girl. "I'm so happy to have you both around I could nearly burst with it." Shadow hugged Autumn. "Welcome to the family, my dear. I'm so glad my Joey found you."

She was too. Her son seemed calmer than he'd ever been. The haunted look was also gone, and she'd seen him smile several times since they'd arrived. Shadow didn't care about the magic or anything else. As far as she was concerned, Autumn could have anything she wanted. She'd managed to get her son to smile again.

Chapter 2

Joey sat by his grandpa's grave. He wasn't one to dwell on what could have happened or should have, but he missed the old man more than he ever thought he would. Picking up an errant leaf, he held it in his hands as he looked at the house he and Autumn were going to be living in.

"Did you know about her too?" He didn't expect an answer and wasn't surprised when none was forthcoming. "She's very calming for me, just like you used to be. All she needs to do is look at me, and I can handle the crowds of people and not have to run out into the yard every few minutes. I wonder if she fishes."

Watching the movers taking the boxes containing her things into the house, he thought about her shooing him away to come here. Looking at the dateless marker on his grandpa's grave, he did smile when he thought of the reason they'd not marked it with the year he'd been born and died. People would have never believed it.

"I've come into my magic. I don't know how much you knew about what happened the night of the robbery, but Tanner and Aurora saved me for you. I now know what you meant when you said that to me all the time. They had saved me for you." The house he grew up in wasn't far from where they were going to live. Joey was glad for that. He wanted to get closer to his mom and dad again. "You've been gone for two years now. Everyone I've spoken to said the day you died, it was like a cloud descended as a constant reminder of how lively you made the place around here. Although Grandpa Oliver is doing a good job now that he's over his grief."

He thought about the night that had brought him and his grandpa Ollie so close. The night of the robbery and his part in it that ended the lives of several people. All of them were bad people from the start, but Joey hadn't heeded his parents' or his grandpa's advice in staying away from them.

"I've never told you this before, but when they tossed me into the trunk of the car, I was hoping for prison. A place where I could be alone. That I'd not see the disappointed look on my parents' faces when I'd walk away from them. Only you understood it wasn't them. It was me. That night, I will never forget what you showed me about what spending my life in prison would have been like. And you told me just how much it would hurt the two people that loved me enough to adopt me and to keep me after everything I'd put them through."

Wiping at the tears he shed for the man he'd been, he put his hand on the grave's marker for the two people there. One he knew better than he knew himself; the other, his grandma. Joey felt as if he knew her too, what with all the stories he'd been told about her.

"I love you, old man. With all my heart. I miss you too, but I know you're where you wanted to be before you took me under your wing." He looked at the house again when he heard his name called. It was Autumn. "I'm sure there will be trouble when her family comes around. I'm also positive I can handle them. But as you reminded me all the time, it's easier to take someone down with help than to have all the battle scars on my body and the memories I can't share."

He got up then, wiping again at his cheeks, and kissed his hand before putting it atop the marker of Oliver Wendall Whitfield, patriarch of the Whitfield family. "I love you."

Making his way to the house, he smiled when Autumn came toward him. She was dressed in a pretty summery dress and a smile that could warm the world. When she was close enough he could touch her, she reached for his hand, and Joey took it. Her smile was all he needed for now.

"Your brother is in the house. Bennett said he's not seen you in years. How is that possible?" He told her he'd been away, trying to find himself. "Did you? Did you find the person you are now or are you still looking, Joey? I want to help you. You've done so much for me that I want to help you in the same ways."

"I think I've found myself. If I didn't, then I found you, and that's more than enough for me." She stared at him. "What do you see when you look at me, Autumn? A regular man or a broken one? I've been broken for so long I'm not sure who I am most of the time."

"I see a man on the verge of something great. Yes, you're hurt, but not broken. Not that you didn't come close at times. I don't know what a regular man is, so I'm going to tell you what else I see." He nodded for her to continue. Joey didn't know what he expected, but the next words out of her mouth surprised him. "A man I've fallen in love with. I don't know when it happened. The day you chased my sister out of the house? Could be, but that's only part of it. The person that saved my life? Him I love a great deal, but that's not what I see either—a fixer. No, what I see is a man that could and will love. That someday, when we're both ready, will be a great father. Understand and have a wealth of information to share with them. You'll keep me safe from myself and those that wish me harm. Even though I could save myself now, it will be up to you to keep me from harm. I do love you, Joey. I will forever, too. Whatever else is going on behind those eyes of yours, it'll work its way out as well. I believe if we're together, then nothing can overcome us."

He kissed her then. Joey had thought he'd just kiss her gently, and they'd go see Bennett, but the kiss warmed his heart, his mind centered on just her. When he lifted his head, breathing hard, he looked at Autumn and fell in love with her too.

Taking her hand, not giving in to the impulse to take her on the ground, they walked to the house he knew as well as he did his own parents' home. The furniture was new, pieces he'd never seen before. But it still had the warmth and hominess he'd always associate with this house. Bennett, coming from the kitchen, nearly leapt at him to hug him.

"Holy Christ, I've missed you. And you come back with a mate. I'll have a bit more catching up to do, I think." Bennett hugged him again as they moved toward the kitchen, where he knew his parents were. "You have a staff here too. I don't know if you were told that or not, but people were lined up to be a part of your family. How have you been?"

He didn't have an answer. How *had* he been? Before he could get too deep into answering the question or not, he asked the cook, Mary Margaret, if there was anything to drink. Glasses of tea—just like he liked it, without sugar—were set before them. Drinking his glass down, he was surprised when Autumn did the same. However, instead of refilling it from the pitcher as he'd thought, both their glasses refilled on their own. Another trick he'd learned and shared with his mate.

"I'm here to stay. Did Mom tell you?" Mom said she was happiest for that bit of news. He looked at his dad, who winked at him when Mom left the kitchen. "Did I upset her?"

"No. She's been teary all afternoon. You should have seen her in the car coming home. She's just so happy to have her boys back together. Bennett has been working hard to make as much trouble as the two of you used to do, but he's fallen short of his goal." Autumn left him to check on his mom. "She said she'd been sick. What was wrong with her?"

"Cancer. It was in her blood and on her brain. The doctors hadn't caught it in time." Dad asked if he'd healed her. "I did. I have a great deal more magic now than before I left home. I guess you could say I've grown into it. Tanner helped me."

"He told us you were trying to control it. That you were even more powerful than he was." Tanner hadn't told him he'd been speaking to his parents. He didn't mind, but he hadn't known. "My parents are coming over later. We didn't tell them you were home, just that we wanted to look around the house for any leaks or anything. Dad, of course, had to complain, but he's missed you as well."

"I've missed everyone." He knew that was true. Even though he'd not thought all that much about his family, he realized he had missed them.

When his mom and Autumn returned, he could

tell they'd both been crying. Mom apologized for leaving. It was Autumn that told her it was an emotional time. When they sat down in the dining room, a room he had a lot of fond memories of, Joey told his parents what was going on with Autumn and her sisters.

"Do you want our help with it?" Before he could tell his dad no, he had it, Autumn answered for him. She said she would want their help. "It's been a while since we've had to help a damsel in destress. Grandpa would have been in his element today, don't you think?"

"He would have taken her under his wing and made sure nothing harmed her." Joey put his arm around Autumn. "I wish you could have met him. He would have loved you very much."

"You should tell your parents what it is you had to get under control. While it's just the four of us." He said later would be better. "No. I think now is a perfect time. They're worried you're not up to par. That you're going to leave them as soon as tomorrow."

When the table started to shake, he looked at it instead of his parents. When Autumn told him again to show them, he felt his temper, something he'd not felt in a very long time, start to rise. When she stood up, he did as well.

"Tell them, or I will. It's important to them both." He asked her why forgetting for a moment that his parents were right there. "They need to know they didn't fail you."

That got him looking at his mom and dad. "You've never failed me. Never in all my life has anyone been there for me like the two of you have been." Mom leaned her head into Dad's chest. "Dad, you don't think that, do you? That you've failed me somehow?"

"Yes. We both do. You've been gone more than you've been here. We can only assume it's because of something we've done. I know you and Tanner both told us you were learning to control your magic. Why didn't you ask us? Why didn't you come to either one of us when you were learning your magic? We would have moved heaven and earth for you, Joey. But it felt like you were forever pushing us away. Again." Joey asked them if they meant at the trial. "I do. You wouldn't allow us to come and see you there. It broke us to know you didn't need us."

"Didn't need you? I was leaving because I thought you'd think I was some sort of freak of nature. Every time I took a breath, I thought of you. Each time a little more magic came to me, I wanted to show you." Mom asked why he'd left them instead of staying. "To protect you."

"From what?" Joey stood up. "Please. I don't think my heart can take it if you leave us again, Joey. If you need to keep this from us, we'll both learn to live with it. But we need you, son. More than we have needed any of our children. We wanted to be there for you, but you pushed us out of your life."

"I'm not leaving." He closed his eyes and thought

of all the things he could do now. All the magic he had at his disposal. Looking at his parents, he asked them if they'd go into the yard with him. "I'll have more room and not destroy the house. I want you to know I'm not leaving. I won't leave you again like I have before. I think…I hope once you see what I've become, you're going to understand why I had to leave you to learn this. All right?"

Joey looked at Autumn when they went to the yard. Pushing her hair off her cheek, he thought of all the things he wanted to say to her. Instead, he told her how much he loved her. Her cheeky grin had him laugh.

"How did I make it through my life without having you by my side to guide and bully me? You knew about their feelings, didn't you?" She said his mom had told her some, but she'd found the rest. "I see. Obviously, you didn't hurt her in searching her mind. I love you, Autumn. Will you be there when they reject me?"

"If they do, they're not nearly as perfect as I think they are now." She cocked her head and looked at him. "Are you aware that your eyes change color? Yesterday they were blue. An hour ago, they were green. Now they're crystal clear. I never know what color they're going to be from moment to moment."

"No, I didn't. I don't usually have a mirror around me when I'm out in the woods." She said she'd be his mirror from now on. "Good. Just don't leave me out there alone. I want them to know, but I'm also afraid. Afraid they really will think of me as a monster."

"Like I said, they're not as nice as you think they are if they do that. Which I don't believe they will. They love you, Joey. And will no matter what comes along. Show them what you've become, and they'll understand more than you can imagine. You also need to tell them why you have such magic. It wasn't just the queen and Tanner. It was all of the world that changed you into what you are." Joey asked her how she had come to that. "I've been speaking with the queen."

When she left him there, he laughed. Joey hadn't laughed this much in a long time, and even to his ears, it was rusty sounding and harsh. He had a feeling he'd get more practice as time went on. Autumn was going to keep him on his toes.

~~~

Blake didn't know what to think about Joey. He loved him, there was never any doubt in that. But he seemed different now, even more so than he had before leaving them for the last two years. While they'd spoken to him in that time, they weren't really conversations so much as him telling them he was still around and he'd be home sooner or later. Blake just knew they'd failed him, as Autumn had said.

Aurora joined them just as Joey and Autumn came out of the house. She smiled at them both and explained that Joey had asked her to be there. And that Autumn had threatened her.

"She's quite the bossy little thing, isn't she? She'll be good for him. Take him to places he's been too afraid to be before this. Not physical places, but places in your family. He's quite right, Blake, when he says he would have hurt you before gaining control." Blake said he would have helped. "I don't believe you would have been able to. Not that you'd not try, but you would have been hurt in ways well beyond what he would have done to all of you physically. He's very strong. The strongest being I've ever seen."

Chairs appeared for them to sit in. Autumn joined them and not only manufactured a chair for herself but also made a small table filled with fresh fruit and glasses of tea. Blake took one of the glasses to keep his hands from shaking. This, he thought, was going to be a test of his strength to remain still.

Blake looked at his son. He'd taken his shirt off, and it hit him how grown up his boy had become. Also, he saw that he'd been marked all over his torso with sigils he'd never seen before. Magic. That was all he could think about. His son was covered in magic.

"When I was five, before coming to live with you and Mom, I helped save a faerie. Her name was Flora. I know you know her. She's one and the same that stayed with Tanner all these years. One of the neighborhood children had caught her and was in the process of tearing her wings off." Blake glanced at Aurora and knew she'd been aware of this. "I saved her. Nursed her back to health with what I could and let her go as soon as she was able to fly again. This is what she granted me for saving her life."

Wings at his back spread out. Blake saw that not only did they tower above his head, but they also pooled along the ground. They were magnificent in color as well as size. Blake's fingers itched to get up and touch them. When Joey moved them twice, he rose from the ground and stayed there for several seconds before he landed softly. The wings disappeared, but Blake knew for some reason that this was only a very little bit of what he was going to learn today.

"Several weeks later, Flora brought me another faerie. She, too, left me a gift of magic. It was for me to produce food for myself. To keep me from starving when I was locked away." He spread out his hands and a table laden with more food than he'd seen, even at Thanksgiving, was in front of them. Blake looked at Joey when he continued. "After a while, I was able to heal even the most harmed of creatures from the earth. I never told anyone of this ability, for I was afraid it was only a dream. That no one would believe me if I told them that faeries, tiny creatures, were brought to me when they'd been tortured by humans."

Blake looked at Aurora. "Did you know all of this?" Aurora shook her head. "Why didn't someone tell you he was helping your people? I'm not upset, but I'd really like to know."

"They thought of him as their friend. Joey had asked them not to tell anyone, and they didn't. They kept their secret from me because he'd helped them and then asked them to do so. It wasn't until he met Flora some years ago that she told me. It was why I was so glad I could return his help when he was locked in the trunk of that car. He needed me, all of us, and we came to his aid."

"Over the years, living with you, I helped a great many creatures. They all were sworn to secrecy, and they kept that promise. I was terrified if you found out what I was doing behind your back, you'd tell me to stop. I wasn't as secure in my love for the two of you as I am now." Blake asked him if he'd healed a bear. "I did. You caught me helping him. I was so afraid you'd beat me then. I knew in my head you'd not, but my heart wasn't as brave as my head was. You never confronted me on it. I did wonder why."

"I didn't believe what I saw, to be honest with you." Blake laughed. "I knew the bear was a wild animal, and I just wrote it off as being my mind playing tricks on me. My goodness. When I think back on some of the wounds you had as a child, you were helping them all along. Right?"

"Yes." Joey glanced at Autumn, then back at him. "I didn't think you'd take this as well as you are. It's like you think it's funny or something."

"Oh, don't get me wrong. I'm ashamed of myself

for not putting two and two together. But I'm about as proud of you as I could have ever been. You not only saved creatures with your magic, Joey, but you did it because you wanted to. Not for the praise or anything else that I, as well as your mom, would have lavished on you. That, my dear boy, makes it all the better for me to hear from you." He nodded once, his emotions getting the better of him. "I love you, Joey. I have and will always love you."

Blake watched his son without any jealously in his heart. He had been, he knew that now, jealous of his grandda for having such a close bond with him. But now that he thought on it, Grandda wasn't doing anything more than protecting Joey. Mostly, he'd bet, from himself. The magic on someone so young would be overwhelming, and he was also coping with his new life with them and terrified of being taken away again.

"There are so many things I can do. I can heal the earth." Autumn told them how he would sit outside in the yard, naked, and repair the earth in places where it was needed. "I need to be naked so all of the earth can speak to me. The world, in some cases, only needs a little help. Flowers planted in areas for animals. Trees grown faster for animals to hide in. Things I can do to give back to all those who helped me."

"When he was hurt, as I said, the earth, not just me, came to his aid. The markings on his body are the marks of friendship and magic. Each mark on him is another leader that thanked him by giving him what he would need to continue helping them." Aurora smiled at him and Shadow. "He's given back more than he's ever taken from the earth. Joey can work with the earth, the wind, and water. Command it in ways that even astound me. He has been, I guess you would call it, created so the earth can be just a little safer with him around."

As minutes and hours went by, Joey showed them things that were outstanding to Blake. Blake never knew, he had no idea Joey was hiding such powers within his body. He understood more than ever why he'd left them to train himself. And Joey was correct too. There wasn't any way he or any of the rest of them could have helped him with such magic. It was more than he'd ever, in all his life, seen on a single body.

They ate from the feast Joey had prepared. It stayed hot the entire time it was out there for them. Plates were magically taken away when they were finished with them. Glasses refilled themselves. Rolls and butter would refill in the basket made for them. Blake could taste the recipes his mother had used all her life, such as the candied carrots he so loved to eat. Joey would know these things, favorites of theirs, and that was why they were in abundance on the table. It really was a feast for them.

Whenever Joey paused for just a moment, Autumn would take him a glass of juice. He'd drink it down and kiss her. Blake had a feeling the kiss he was getting was helping him as much if not more than the juice was. Liking the young woman more and more, he was glad when she told Joey it was enough for the day.

"You're exhausted. You can show off again tomorrow, but for today, you need to rest." Joey told her he wasn't really that tired. "Well, I'm sure they are. They've been sitting in those chairs for over four hours. They need to rest their butts, even if you don't."

She was a bossy little thing, as he'd been told. But there was more to her than being bossy. She was a caring individual that had brought their son home to them. As surely as he was sitting there, Blake knew Joey wouldn't have come home again right now if it hadn't been for her. He owed her a great debt of gratitude.

Dad and Mom showed up just as they were entering the house. Mom burst into tears at seeing Joey there, and his dad hugged him as Mom scolded Joey for being gone so long. Dad sniffled a little as he introduced himself to Autumn.

"Are you the young lady I have to thank for having my grandson come home?" Autumn, in her usual way, Blake thought, told his dad he didn't have to thank her for anything. "Snippy thing, aren't you? I don't care. You and he, you're here for good then? I'd like to tell you we all knew you'd be coming home. I'm gladder than I've been about anything that you've come here together."

"We are too. I have some issues with my sisters, but I'm not really worried about them anymore like I used to be." Autumn looked at Joey, and Blake could feel her love for him as if it were a tangible thing. "He saved me. Not just my life, though that is wonderful, but he saved me from being alone. I didn't know I was until I met him."

Blake and his family hung out with the two of them till well past midnight, each telling something of their life. He learned Autumn was magical in her own right before meeting Joey. He also learned that Tanner had been granted the ability to stay in the sunlight. But Joey said he felt badly about doing that to him.

"When I see him again, I'm going to take it back. He's been more than helpful for me, and like Grandpa Ollie, he's tired of this earth and wishes to move on." There was a moment of sadness then. Thinking of his grandda's last day still hurt him when he thought about it. Which he still did daily, but not every second of every hour. Grandda Ollie was a good man and was missed by all. But too, he'd been an old man when he'd been given immortality, and his body still ached with the age he'd been.

On their way back to their home, he and Shadow talked about how good it was to have Joey home. They also spoke about how much they loved Autumn. They both realized she was going to be caring for Joey more than he would her. She had their son right where he needed to be. Home and accepted.

"Autumn understands him on a level we would

never have been able to achieve. He was right to go away to understand himself." Blake said he knew that as well. "Had we forced him to, I think he would have stayed, but his heart would never have mended like it has now. We would have been too focused on keeping him the way we wanted him to be rather than allowing him to be what he is."

"You're right." He laughed when they pulled into the driveway of their home. "How did I get so very lucky in having such a brilliant mate?"

"You were lucky. By now, you shouldn't be surprised by my brilliance anymore." She kissed him as they entered their house. "Oh, this house, it feels so much like a home again. My babies are here. I have a new daughter-in-law. Who knows? Perhaps I'll be a grandmother again soon."

The first thing Blake thought of was being able to hold one of Joey's children. Then it occurred to him that he didn't know what sort of power the children would have. Being born of such beings would be something, he thought. Would it be as powerful as they were? More so? It bore thinking about. But he really did want to hold Joey's child. To see the young man that had had so much happen to him become a father. Smiling as he followed his wife to bed, he wondered what sort of mother Autumn would make. Laughing when he entered the bedroom, he swallowed hard.

"I thought I'd show you what a grandmother looked

like." She was naked. Not only that, but she was wearing heels, his favorite thing in the world to see Shadow in. He was glad she'd beaten him to the room. Closing the door and locking it behind him, Blake decided he'd show her how much strength a grandda had too.

Chapter 3

While May loved her sisters, with the exception of Autumn, she did hate to be caught someplace where they all were. Like today. They were eating in a restaurant she'd suggested, but they didn't come alone. July had her infant, which she supposed was all right. Once a bottle was put in its mouth, it was just fine. July had her two children, the worst children she'd ever been around, May thought. They never ate anything unless they could smash it between their fingers first. Then after that, they covered the ungodly mess with a bottle of ketchup. Nasty stuff that.

Today September told them that she was going to have another baby. Why she wanted to populate the world with more children was beyond her. She already had five of the little creatures. Having more was just too much for her to think about. May told her that too.

"Another child? Good Lord, September, you can

barely keep up with the others. Why on earth didn't you rid yourself of that thing before now? I have the perfect doctor that can do it for you if you want his number." September told her she was just fine with having another child. "You would be. I have no idea how Roy even comes home with all the noise they make. You're just stupid if you ask me."

"I didn't. And I'll thank you to keep your mouth shut about it, too. Besides, we're not here to talk about my having a child. We're here because you have a burr up your ass about Autumn. Why the hell don't you leave her alone? What has she ever done to you that makes you want to kick her around so much?" May told her she'd gotten the house. "Uncle Ross's home? You're still having a fit about that? She can have it as far as I'm concerned. It's nothing but a shack anyway. Not to mention too small for any of us to live in. With the exception of you, of course. You're the only one that hasn't had any children. You want to go and live there, May? Might do you some good to see how the other half lives."

If they only knew how close she was to living just like their sister was. After some bad investments, her spending habits, as well as a high mortgage payment, she was about as broke as she could be. Her husband had left her too. Not that any of them had liked him, but he'd had enough of her micromanaging him every day. He could have said something before deciding she was a pain in his ass and left her, she thought.

She supposed left her wasn't quite right. He'd waited until she'd gone out for the day, then had someone come in and change the locks on the place. When she'd returned, her key, of course, no longer working, a man leapt out at her and handed her a blue file. After telling her she'd been served, she opened it to find Harvey was divorcing her. *He* was divorcing *her*. Fucker.

"What are your plans for her? Run her out of town? Do you want someone to kill her? Those might be all well and good for you, but since she's not bothered me, I'm with September. Leave her alone." May needed a few moments to remember what they'd been talking about and asked June how she could say something like that. "Easily. She's got the house that was falling down around Uncle Ross's ears before he died. I'm sure there is little left to make it worth anything. I don't want anything from the place or her. Just leave her alone."

"Well, I, for one, am with you, May. I was out there recently to see if she'd died or something. For only having a month to live, she certainly has stretched it well out beyond what I would have thought." She asked April what she'd done. "I did get in, but I'm sure she's changed the locks again since then. But to be honest with you, I will never go back there. She had a large lion there. And don't tell me I've got it wrong. I still have nightmares every time I think about how close he came to ripping my throat out."

May rolled her eyes. It might well have been a

large cat, the domestic kind. That was something they all knew about April. She tended to overstate things. Even if one of them was there with her, she'd swear it was what she said.

"I'm going out there as soon as we're finished here. I have a few things I'd like to say to her myself." May thought of the man that had been out there with her sister, who July had told her about. She was going to have a conversation with him as well. He was just some sort of servant or nurse, that was for sure. Christ knew what her sister was paying him. "If you want to go with me, then tell me now. I wanted all of us to go there, but it seems that some of you have been away from her for too long to remember what she did to us."

"What did she do to us? I'm the youngest, just below her. I don't remember her doing anything other than trying to survive us." June huffed before speaking again. "None of us were all that nice to her. Especially Mom and Dad." February told her with good reason too. "What reason? I'd really like to know why you've held onto this grudge for so long."

"I don't have time to go over her misdeeds. Isn't it bad enough for you that she had all that magic and didn't share it?" June asked her how that was supposed to work. None of them were the seventh in anything. "Okay, not share, but she could have done more for us. Like helping with the house. Did you know she could have cleaned the entire thing with just a snap of her fingers?"

"As far back as I can remember, the house was forever cleaned up. I don't remember having to take out the trash or even wash the dishes. I don't think any of us had to." June pretended to think on it. "Nope. None of us did a thing to help out around the house other than to leave without making our beds. We never picked up our clothing, and I don': remember ever once having to put away our laundry. Now that you mention it, we didn't do shit around there. Not even yard work. She did it, I'm betting."

May was sure she had too. Not only had Autumn kept the house cleaned up, and the yard mowed when necessary, but she also made sure the neighbors had nice yards. Their driveways were plowed in the winter months. Even their flowers were neatly planted and happy looking.

After lunch, where she'd been able to con one of them into paying her check, she went to the bathroom and looked at herself in the mirror. Fighting age was difficult, she thought. Forever having to make sure no gray hairs were present, that wrinkles didn't mar her skin. Something else she'd hated Autumn for was her perfect self. She'd never had acne when she was a teenager. Autumn had stayed slim her entire life, well into adulthood. No matter what she ate, May had to work out to remove the unwanted fat. Autumn's hair, a wonderful shade of deep red, had never looked out of sorts. Even when she was awakened in the morning, her hair looked just as pretty as it had when she fell asleep.

Autumn had had good grades in school, too, good enough to have gotten a full scholarship to any college she wanted to go to. She did, too, going to college and graduating at the top of her class like she had in high school. There was nothing flawed about their sister. She was fucking perfect in every conceivable way.

When they were on their way to the house, May was hurt the others hadn't gone with her—just January, February, and July. June didn't want anything to do with any of it. September was too busy having enough children to put the world in crisis.

May looked in her mirror when July told her she'd missed the turnoff. "I did not. I know where to turn. Where the house is sitting out by the road." July told her she'd missed it according to her phone, and she should turn around. "I'll turn around when I'm damned good and ready."

That was another thing her husband said—she had a closed mind. If she had closed her mouth as much as she did her mind to new things, they might well have gotten along better. As it was, he didn't want to have to debate every little thing he told her. Now here she was doing it again with her sisters.

After another fifteen minutes of driving, she did turn around, but she refused to believe she'd done anything wrong. The pull off where the house should have been was nothing but weeds as if nothing had been there in decades rather than just a few days ago. The house, a tiny little thing that was really falling down, wasn't anywhere to be seen. Each of them got out and walked to where the pathway had been their entire lives.

"Well, this is where it's supposed to be." Not only did they kick around the grass, looking for any kind of clue as to what happened, May drove to the neighbor's home and asked her where the house had gone. "My sister was very ill, and now I can't find her home. Surely nothing happened to it. Did it?"

May hoped not. It was going to have to house her until she got her husband to take her back. Or failing that, she needed to find herself another man with money. May swore she'd be better with money this time. She'd only buy things on sale. No more buying just to be buying.

"You mean that little house Autumn lived in? I don't know. I've not thought about it being gone. I do know some young man came by to tell me he and Autumn were moving to his home. I didn't think to ask her where she'd be going. Nice young man too. I hope she's happy. After you six, I'm sure she deserves it." May asked her what that was supposed to mean. "You know just what I'm talking about, young lady. Ross, he told me all about how you treated that little sister of yours. To think the seven of you came from the same genes. Never a nicer neighbor I've ever had. If she's happy, then you should just leave her alone. You got no reason to be bothering her anymore."

"I have plenty of reasons. If she or Uncle Ross badmouthed us, then she's going to tell you the truth." The woman, older than she was, told her she knew the truth as much as May did. "I haven't any idea what you're going on about. I only came here to check on the whereabouts of my sister. She's ill, you know."

The woman laughed. "So not only have you lost your sister's home, but her too. My goodness, you're not having a very productive day, now are you?"

She was still cackling as she went back into her home. The smell of berry pies or something came through the open window when the door opened to allow the old woman into her home. May's mind was flooded with memories of the same smells coming from her own home as a child. Autumn again. She'd say she got them some berries for pie or something. May could remember eating more than her share simply so Autumn couldn't have any. The stupid girl never said a word to her about it either.

As they drove back to town and to the police station, she thought of all the stupid things Autumn had done. She never told on any of them when they were mean to her or hurt her. Mostly it was her and January, but they never got into trouble. After a while, it wasn't as much fun as it used to be at the beginning. It was because when Autumn told on them, she was the one that got punished, not them. When she kept her mouth shut, Mom and Dad would still punish her, but not because of them. It got to be boring watching her baby sister being treated as she'd been. And Autumn did get punished.

Almost as if she'd read her mind, July spoke up about the worst punishment Autumn had gotten. "You remember when Mom looked up how to make paint stripper? Did you know she was going to force it down Autumn's throat?" May said she'd helped make it. "I didn't ask you if you made it, May. I asked if you knew then that Mom was going to pour it down her throat? To make her drink it?"

"No. I didn't know." That had been horrific. Watching her drink down the liquid only to puke it back up. The more she puked it up, the more Mom would pour down her throat until she was throwing up nothing but blood. "I thought she was finally going to paint our bedroom. I don't remember what Autumn did to deserve that. I'm sure if I think on it, I'll—"

"She didn't do anything. She never had to do anything to be hurt like that. But making her drink that shit. That has haunted me. Not all the time, but when I'd think of her. Autumn, she wasn't a bad kid. Just different than us." May didn't have a single answer to her sister's comment. "Autumn never lived with us after that. I mean, she was in the hospital for a very long time, but she never came home. Did she?"

"No. Not even at the holidays." There hadn't been any stopping of Mom and Dad, however. They just centered their meanness on the town they'd lived in. Never any of them. Never their children. The town suffered badly after Autumn left home. "Do you remember how old she was? She might have been like ten or something if I remember."

"When Mom poisoned her? I have to think on it." If she ever remembered, July didn't tell her. Mom had forever tried to kill off Autumn. Not just with the poisons, but with knives and an axe once. May remembered a time when their dad had tied a noose around Autumn's neck and tried dragging her through the fields. She never complained to any of them. Not, now that she thought about it, that it would have done her any good. Her sisters didn't like her simply because their parents didn't.

The police station house was busy. Shift change, May thought. Going inside, the police snickered, and she looked around to see what they thought was so funny. May could use a good laugh about now. But instead, she found them all looking at her.

"What are you laughing about?" None of them would look at her then. Going up to the desk, she asked the man there if she could talk to an officer. "I need to know where my sister is."

"Gone." She asked the man where she'd gone. "She didn't tell me. She and a man came in yesterday and said she was going to go live with him. Also, she mentioned she was getting married. Never seen her so happy before. Why don't you just leave her alone? She's not bothering any of you."

"In the event it might have slipped your mind, my sister is very ill. This man, for all you know, could be swindling her out of her money." The man laughed and said he doubted he would need anything to do with her money. "Oh? And you know this how? Is she marrying some rich bastard that will supply her with all kinds of things? Get real. No one wants to take on an ill person like she is."

"She didn't look ill when she was here, to be honest with you, May. She looked healthy as I've ever seen her. Happy too, like I said." May didn't want to hear about her health or the man she was supposed to be marrying. He was going to be a deadbeat, she just knew it. "What else can I help you with?"

"Who tore down the house?" The officer, she didn't know his name, asked her what she meant. "The house. It's not there. I was going to stay in it while she was gone. Now I can't seem to find it. What happened that it had to be torn down?"

"Well, now, if I have all my information right, her future husband, he said he was going to take care of it. Said Autumn didn't want any squatters in her uncle's house. You have her permission to be living there, May? I'm thinking not, or she would have mentioned that to me as well." She asked him if he'd just called her a squatter. "I guess I did. You just go on back to wherever it is you came from. You and those sisters of yours. I'm warning you right now, May, none of you want to mess with that man she's hitching herself up to. Or any of his family for that matter."

"Oh? And why is that? Is he something special? The president or something? Perhaps he's not quite that good, but the governor or something?" The man just laughed. "Well, what is it that makes him so special?"

"One of his uncles was the president for a while. I believe he served several terms too. Adrian Whitfield was his name. Uncle to Joey, the man your sister is marrying. Also, as for governor? Well, I think a few of them have been in the position too. I know Joey's grandda was the mayor for a while. I think he's retired by now. One of his other grandkids is doing the job, I think." Whitfield? She was marrying a Whitfield? May had to sit down and realized she might have missed something the man was telling her. He was fanning her now with a file that had been on his desk. She only just noticed it had her name on it. Snatching it from him, she opened it up and saw her picture there. "Your husband, I'm sure you're aware he's changed the locks on the house and that you're not welcome there anymore. I think he's also planning to divorce you. Serves you right for being the bitch you've been."

If there was more, she didn't hear it. Staggering her way back out to her car, it took her several tries to get into it. Once she was inside, she could only sit there. Starting her car seemed to be impossible. May didn't know where to start. Looking around, hoping to have one of the others go inside and verify what she'd only just heard, she realized they'd left her. May was alone in the car.

Laying her head on the steering wheel, May realized two things. Her sister was marrying into the richest family in the world. Secondly, they would protect her with their lives. The Whitfields were, just as the officer told her, not people to fuck with. How was she ever going to get a place to live now that her sister was off limits to her?

~~~

Joey wasn't sure what to do with himself. He knew where he'd been sleeping when he stayed all night with his grandpa, but with Autumn in the house, he hadn't any clue what she wanted. Sitting in the office, the one he'd sat at millions of times when he'd come here, Joey looked around.

The books on the shelves had all been read by him. At first, Grandpa had read them to him, then after a little while, he'd read them back to him. Grandpa Oliver had been there helping him learn as well. Since he'd not been very good around people, the two men homeschooled him until he could take college classes online and graduate from there. Thanks to the old men, he not only had a better education than most people his age, but he also had a well rounded view of businesses and stock markets.

When Autumn joined him, he asked her if she was

getting things squared away all right.

"I am. Your mom told me you've taken over running your grandparents' businesses. That you were a whiz at investments and such. I was wondering if you'd like to take over our gem business." He asked her if she was sure. "Yes. I trust you if that's what you meant."

"No. I mean, I'm happy you trust me, but do you want me to have a hand in your family's company?" She frowned at him. "Come here. I want to show you something."

The computer was forever on, but waking it up took a few seconds. When she sat on his lap, it was all he could do not to beg her to take him. To tell her she was in a dangerous spot if she didn't want to make love with him.

"The program I use for investments is older than this one. I think it's the same one Uncle Ross used when he had his pension moved around." He told her he always had the newest versions of programs, thanks to his family. "So do you invest the money from the profit, or do you take the money you have already and invest?"

They spent the next hour going over where the money was coming from, how he decided what was going to move to another account, and what he had to hold onto. Joey suggested that she upgrade her programs and try to see if she liked it better. When she leaned back against his shoulder, he kissed her on the head and thought about living the rest of his days with her at his side.

"I've something to tell you." He said he was there for her. "I've never enjoyed sex. I've had it a couple of times, and I found it to be not just messy, but sort of boring."

Joey couldn't help it, he burst out laughing. "Of all the things I thought you were going to tell me, that wasn't even on the radar." Turning her around, so she was sitting on his lap facing him, he looked at her beautiful face and decided to tell her something too. "I was sexually abused as a child. Not here. This was the only place I was able to heal and figure out that hugs didn't come with a punch to the gut. Kisses led to nothing except knowing how much you missed or loved someone. And best of all, I found out that not everyone is as bad as my biological parents were. While I've had sex, like you, I've never been all that thrilled with it. However, I think the two of us will not just enjoy it, but realize that making love is so much different than having sex with someone."

When she rolled her hips forward, Joey closed his eyes. Begging him to look at her, Joey watched her emotions through her eyes. She was the most beautiful creature he'd ever seen. Putting his hands on her hips, he pulled her forward and removed her clothes. Making himself as naked as she was, he suckled at her breasts until she pleaded with him for more.

"We can go to the bedroom if you want." She shook her head and told him to take her. Clearing the desk was easy — parting with her body to lay her out on his desk was much harder. "Please. Take me. I need to come before we can make love slowly."

He didn't so much enter her but slammed forward. She was wet and warm. Her body welcomed him like a hand to a glove. Stilling his movements to make sure he didn't come before her, Joey nearly cried out when her sheath started to milk him. His cock, hard as stone, seemed to have a mind of its own, and Joey leaned over her while he took her hard enough to move the heavy desk across the room.

The need to fill her nearly took his breath away. She held him tightly, her legs wrapped around his hips, her arms around his neck. Joey leaned into her throat, smelling her scent that was her call to him. When she cried out that she was coming, Joey had no choice but to follow her over the edge.

Both of them were breathing hard when he pulled her off the desk and into the chair with him. His cock was still hard, but not painfully so. As soon as she looked up at him, her eyes full of need, Joey took them to their bedroom and laid them both out on the big bed.

"I love you." She smiled at him, telling him she loved him more. "Doubtful, but I'm all right with that. I want to make love to you. See your face when you come again."

They made love to each other then, him touching places that made her sigh, kissing skin as soft as a rose petal. Joey discovered he was ticklish under his chin. He found out that Autumn loved to have her nipples suckled. Making love to her, with her, Joey discovered he was a romantic after all. That making her come over and over was what made his heart fill and spill out into the rest of his body.

Joey came so many times, short punches to his system that, instead of calming him, giving him relief, seemed to energize him in some way. He was in love, making love to the only woman he would ever love.

When she came again, screaming out his name and her love for him, Joey joined her once again. The bright spots behind his eyelids had him hold her tighter to himself. The pictures, because that was what they looked like, flashed there just long enough for him to see them, but nothing more.

There was no rhyme or reason to them. He was holding a child in one. A stone marker that bore the name Whitfield was there as well. A house on fire. A gun lying in a pool of blood. Finally, when they stopped flashing, he was left with a single picture of a couple sitting on a porch, swinging on a hanging swing. Then nothingness.

When he woke, he had no clue as to how long he'd been out. But as Autumn was sleeping beside him, his body spooned around hers, he knew it couldn't have been all that long. Pulling her closer, Joey pulled the blanket up and over the two of them. Inhaling deeply, he wondered if he'd ever get used to the smell of Autumn.

He hoped not. Closing his eyes, he fell back to sleep until a voice was in his mind.

Joey? He didn't move when his mom called for him. *Joey, I need for you to wake up. A woman by the name of September Hasher is at our house. She's looking for Autumn. I guess the sisters had a falling out yesterday, and September wants to tell Autumn about it.*

The shower was on when he sat up. His mom was talking fast, and he was only getting about every other word from her. Asking her to slow down, he knew, was rude, but he had been so asleep he needed a few more minutes to wake.

Autumn is in the shower. Is she armed? September? Mom told him that she hadn't found any weapons on her. *I've never met but a couple of them. I think this one isn't so bad. Has a lot of children.*

She's going to have another one too if I don't miss my bet. Are you coming here, or do you want us to come over there? Joey, she seems harmless. But there are marks on her that make me think she's been knocked around a little. Could be nothing more than her having a couple of kids under feet all the time. Do you think they'd hurt each other over Autumn? He told her he didn't know, but he'd have to ask Autumn what she wanted to do. *You do that, then let me know. As I said, she seems harmless. Before I forget to tell you again, Dylan has done a background check on all of them. I'll give it to the two of you when you tell me where to go with this.*

Staggering to the bathroom, smiling because

he'd been so worn out from last night, he knocked on the bathroom door and heard Autumn tell him she was almost finished. He told her he'd just spoken to his mom and what she had to say. When the water went off, he waited on her.

"September is pregnant again too. Also, my Aunt Dylan has done some background checks on your family. She said she'd give it to you when you get there, or they come here. Whichever you decide, honey, I'm behind you all the way." Autumn asked him what he'd do. "Meet her here, on your own grounds. Serve her tea or whatever she drinks. Make it seem as if you don't have a care in the world where she's concerned."

"I like that." She reached for the towel and winced a little. "My muscles are tender today. I'm betting you don't feel a thing, do you?"

"I had to sit on the side of the bed for five minutes before I could move in here to talk to you. And even with that, I staggered like an old drunk man. I feel every muscle in my body, and I'm laying blame at your feet." Laughing with him, Autumn told him to tell his mom here was great. After talking to his mom, he told Autumn what she said. "An hour should be enough time for me to shower and get some of the kinks out of my body. If you'd not mind telling Mary Margaret we're to have guests, she can whip something up for all of us."

He stood under the spray for several minutes before reaching for the shampoo. Joey really was sore, but he'd do it all over again even if he would have been twice as sore. Smiling, he took his cues from Autumn and dressed in a pair of jeans and an old T-shirt. He didn't know these people and didn't want to give them the impression he cared about them. Until he figured out who was who and which was going to be the one he had to kill to make certain they knew he was going to protect his mate with his life.

Chapter 4

September didn't hardly recognize her sister. She had always been slim, but now she looked model thin and just as beautiful. The man that had come into the room before her sister had warned her to be nice or he'd kill her. He'd not raised his voice, nor did he drop the nice smile he'd had on his face. Joey had simply welcomed her to their home and said, either be nice, or I'll kill you. Just like he was asking her if she wanted any sugar with her tea. September believed him too. There would be no build up to it. He would just kill her.

"September, if you're here to tell me I owe you something or you want me to do something insane for you, I'm not in the mood. I've only just gotten married, I'm happy as I've ever been, and I don't want any more bullshit from my family. Tell me what you want from me so I can tell you no, and you can be on your way." September just stared at her. "Or you can sit here and look like some sort of druggy."

"No. I mean, wow, you've certainly grown a set." September laughed. "I don't want anything from you. Nor do you need to…what has May said to you? It must have been nasty, knowing her. I've come to warn you about the others. I got to come here instead of June. She wanted to, but she's working today."

"Warn me about what?" A beautiful tea trolly was brought into the room. Even from where she was sitting, September could smell the freshness of the pretty scones and cookies on a plate. The teapot, a beautiful and delicate thing, had four matching teacups and an honest to goodness pot of sugar lumps. "Would you like a cup? Or something else? I'm sure we have whatever it is you wish."

"No. Please. I would love to be served a cup of tea. I so love it in old movies when they enjoy a cup of tea while plotting. Oh, Autumn, I'm so happy for you." September could tell Autumn was shocked by what she said. Good, she thought. She didn't want to be the only one that was shocked. "I have five children now — one on the way too. May has none and thinks every child in the world is going to be a heathen. I have no idea why she's like that. Bitter old bitch."

Joey laughed, and September did see her sister smile. "I don't mean to be rude again, but why are you here? You seem so different than you did when we were growing up. I remember you as being much like the rest of them towards me."

"Yes. I will admit now that I wasn't much of a sister to you. June and I, we get together without the rest of them and talk about our family. Not just you, but all of us growing up. May is so bitter, like I said. I remember her being like that even after you were hurt so badly and nearly killed by our parents. The one thing I remember so well about you as a child was how simply beautiful you were. You still are." Taking a small sip of her tea, September moaned at the lovely delicate taste of it. Taking a small bite of the scone, she looked at her little sister. "After the police came to the house and arrested Mom and Dad, we were taken into foster care. I was with a wonderful family. That was when I realized a person didn't treat children like you were treated. I don't even know why I was...I do hope someday you can forgive me for going along with them. I'm not making excuses, but I will say that had our parents even once in a while stepped in to care for you, I might well have changed my mind about them sooner."

"I don't know why they hated me. Now they're both in prison, I'm not going to go there and find out either. Uncle Ross left what he did to me simply because I'm the one that took care of him as he lay dying. It wasn't an easy death for him." September told her she'd not even known he was ill until she read his obit in the paper. "He was a good man. He treated me well. I had a roof over my head and clothing to wear. Not once did he ever hurt me or take me outside to stand in the cold until I nearly died."

"I'm so sorry, Autumn." She looked around the house and thought how much being rich suited her. "I'm so proud of you too. Having a lovely home. A loving family and husband. I'm happy as well. Once I started standing up for myself with the others, I began to see all kinds of things I'd not before. How mean the others are, even to each other. May is the worst of them. If you want to know the truth, I'm broke. I don't have anything other than what we need. But the difference is, I don't care. My husband could be working at a higher paying job, but he'd not be able to go to soccer games as well as hang out with us. To me, that's much more important than having everything in the world you think you want."

"Did you know May's husband left her?" No, she hadn't, but it would be something May would have driven him to do. Putting down her cup, she was excited to see that Autumn refilled it for her. That meant she wasn't being pushed out the door. "I have all sorts of information on all of you. You included. You're not just broke, September, but you're going to lose your house soon if you don't get caught up. Please don't lie to me again."

"I wasn't lying to you. I am happy. I did say I was broke too." September wanted to be angry with her sister for knowing that much about her situation. But she also knew she had no right to be angry with anyone after the way they'd all treated her. "May and the other three are going to come out here soon. Well, someplace. I don't know that she knows where you live. There are a lot of Whitfields in the area."

She had tried for a joke, but it failed her. Standing up, she told her sister she needed to get home. Autumn stood up as well but did ask her to please sit down and that she was sorry. Tears filled her eyes as she sat back down. Autumn, even after all this time, was still just as sweet and nice as she'd ever been.

"I didn't want to bring my personal troubles here with me. I don't know how you found out, but I think I'm glad you did. I want nothing from you, Autumn, with the exception of a second chance for us to be sisters again. June does as well. She and I want to hang out with you. Have our children get to know you. Us too." She pulled a very worn tissue from her purse. "I'm sorry. I cry at the silliest things nowadays."

"I want to help you get out of the hole." September told her she'd be all right. "No, you won't. When you have to take some time off to have this little girl, you're going to be— What is it?"

"It's a girl? You know that?" Autumn told her it was, and she also knew her exact date of birth. "You can do that too? Oh, Autumn, I've so wanted a girl after having little boys. Just someone I could put pretty dresses on. To take to teas if she'll allow it."

"She might not." September wasn't even trying to

hide her tears now. Sobbing at the fact it was a daughter, she told her sister she loved her. "If that's true, then you'll allow me to help you. To make sure you're not homeless when she comes along. You can call it a loan if you wish, but I don't need you to pay me back. Just please, as your sister, let me help you."

She thought of how bad it was at home. How they only had meat twice a week because it was so expensive. How school fees weren't paid. That her children needed new shoes and coats. When Autumn laughed, September asked her what was funny.

"I can read your mind. I thought I'd take a peek to see what sort of other things you were behind in. Not once did you think of yourself in what extra money could do for you but your children. If you don't allow me to help you now, I'm going to do it anyway. You only thought of the people that depend on you. That, I can get behind." She started crying again. When arms wrapped around her, September felt something she'd never thought to feel from one of her siblings. Love. Understanding too. "Come on. We'll get this fixed up for you, and then we can have dinner together. Will your husband and children be able to come here? If not, we can send a car for them. Call June too. I'd like to see her again if she's able to come."

It took two phone calls for money to be put in her account. September didn't ask her how much it was—just enough, she hoped, not to lose the house. The rest they could take care of if they had a home to live in. Roy was delighted to come to dinner with them. The boys too. She told him three times to make sure they were cleaned up. He laughed when she told him someone was coming to get them. Hanging up the phone after being given a few minutes to call her husband, she called her sister.

"She really wants me and my family to come over? Really? Oh, September. I'm so glad you went to see her. I would have surely mucked it up." September told her she had cried about stupid and silly things. Then told her about the trolley and the cups. "I would have been sobbing the moment the tea cart was brought out. Oh yes, I'll be there. And with my children. Are you sure she wants us to converge on her all at one time? That's a lot."

"She said for me to call you and invite you. Wait until you see her, June. She's just as beautiful inside as she is outside. And her husband is a good looking man." She told June about May's husband.

"We should invite him with us sometime. He more than likely has a great deal to say about May."

"I don't doubt it. Well, I'd better tell her you're all coming. I warned Roy several times to make sure the boys were cleaned up." She laughed and thought about telling her sister she was having a little girl but didn't want to jinx it. "I can't believe how welcoming she's been, June. I have to admit, I thought for sure she'd turn me away without a word."

September didn't tell her about the money either. She didn't want her to think she'd only come out here for some cash. That was the furthest thing from her mind when she girded up her loins and made her way out here.

As she hung up the phone, she looked around the office she was in. There were no pictures on the walls, no mementos of their childhood. As she stood there looking at the things on the shelves, small geodes and larger ones, she realized she'd never seen a picture of her little sister. Not even a birth picture. Walking around the room, she saw pictures of Joey's family. Wedding pictures with him in a tux. Pictures of Christmas with children all over the place.

There were several pictures of an elderly man that obviously meant a great deal to Joey. Taking the picture of Joey and the elderly man down to look closer at it, Joey spoke from behind her.

"My great grandfather. He was the only man in the world that seemed to understand me. He died a few years back. I miss him a great deal." She put the framed picture back and turned to him. "She's crying. I'm not saying that to you because you upset her, but I wanted you to know she's afraid and excited that you've come here."

"Why is she afraid?" Joey asked her to have a seat as he explained it to her. "I guess I can understand her distrust of us. I know I wouldn't have been as open armed as she has been for me. We didn't exactly have a good role model for parents and how to treat children."

"You've done a good job with yours. I'm to

understand you have a gifted child." She nodded and felt her pride put a smile on her face. "I'd like to help you with that as well. I know you've talked to schools that would like to take him there as a student. My parents are on the board there. I can ask them to put in a word or two for you. Also, there would be no cost to you and your—"

"I can't ask you to do that, Joey. I mean, I'd love to, but it's very expensive, and I'd have no way of paying you back on that." He just smiled at her. September had a sudden thought. "You've already made the arrangements, haven't you?"

"I have. Yes. As I said when we were making arrangements for your checking account, we have more than enough money that helping you won't hurt us at all. Also, you should know I'm extremely magical." She asked him if he'd gotten it from Autumn. "No. I've gotten some from her, but mostly it's all mine. I have powers yet to be discovered. Also—this is an ability I've had for some time—I'm able to make those that mean a great deal to us immortal. A person that will be able to be with us until they no longer wish it."

She glanced at the pictures of the elderly man, then back at him. There was a sadness to Joey she'd not noticed before. It had only been noticeable since he'd talked about his great grandda. September asked him about the man.

"He was elderly when the immortality was given to him. So much so he still had the aches and pains of his age. Also, he missed his lady love, as he called her. Grandpa was the only man I ever trusted, with the exception of my father and grandfather, and Grandpa just wanted to die. He died the day I left home in order to find myself. I knew he was going to do it, but I couldn't make myself be here for it. I do regret that more with each passing day." She told him she was sorry. "As am I. There are things I would also like to speak to you about. Things that pertain to May. She's violent. Were you aware of that? Also, she visits her parents weekly, taking them things and money so they don't have to do without. She thinks it's wrong they were imprisoned."

"I knew she visited them. Not that often, but I did know. She has tried to get the rest of us to go. I think June and I are the only two holdouts. As for her being violent? Yes, I was aware that she was as a teenager, but I didn't know she still was. Who has she hurt? I mean, recently?"

He only had to nod, and she understood. Not the who, but that it was more than one person. She looked around the office again, giving herself a few minutes to think about what she wanted to say. There wasn't a place in her heart she didn't hurt for Autumn.

"When we were children, I never understood why my parents hated Autumn so much. Even as an adult, I still don't understand. They would do things to her. Unspeakable things that it never occurred to me were terrible." She thought about that for a moment. "That's not true. I knew they were wrong. But at the time, I was only thinking of myself. I didn't want the same things done to me that were being done to her. Then, after we were taken away, I realized a great many things. Things I'm sure every child knows. Mostly it's that our parents were lazy fucks who only gave a shit about themselves. I also began to think about May and the others. How they were so indoctrinated about how things should go. Money was a biggy. If we had it, so did our parents. If we didn't, we were the greatest disappointments that ever walked the face of the earth. And for whatever reason, they'd take their anger out on Autumn. I wish I could have a do-over with my childhood. But since I can't, I'm going to be the best sister I can to Autumn and June. Also, the best mother I can be."

"I believe you." She thanked him, knowing it was a good start on her relationship with this man. "Your husband is coming here today, and my parents are going to offer him a good job. If you need to, talk him into it, please. He'll be home nightly and on weekends. Also, and I'm glad to know this is something you think about a great deal, he'll be able to take time off for projects, skip a day, or anything you or your children need. My parents have always put family first. My entire family is like that."

"Thank you, Joey. You've done so much for me. I don't know how I will ever repay your kindness." He told her not to hurt his wife. "Never if I can help it. I will die before I hurt her again with intentions."

"That's all I can hope for." He started to leave the grand office but paused at the doorway. "Don't find yourself alone with May or July. Ever. If you do, you'll be hurt. Not killed, not anymore. But they will harm you. And keep your children close."

He left her there before she could ask him what he knew. But then, as she sat there thinking about it, she had a feeling she didn't want to know. If May or July hurt one of her family, there would be nothing in this world that would stop her from killing them both. And she'd gladly go to prison for it.

~~~

Joey hadn't wanted to enjoy the night. He did want it to go well, but he was surprised at how much he enjoyed the children. He liked Roy and Mike as well. They were good men who loved their family as much as he did. Both men, however, were down on their luck, and it looked like the only way they were going to get out of it was with some major changes to their lives.

Mike was a funny man. He was a good father, watching over his sons like they were going to be snatched away from him at any second. When he'd shaken hands with both of them, he knew Mike only had about a year to live. Roy less than that. Mike had prostate cancer that he'd only just found out about. Without insurance, the man was going to suffer needlessly with it. Joey also knew Roy was going to be killed, murdered soon, but he didn't know the details or who would kill him.

"I'd like to offer you a way out. Both of you. My mom is going to offer you a job, Roy, and I'd very much like you to think about taking it." He told him he had a job. "Yes. But you can do better. You only have that job so you can be with your children whenever they need you. I find that commendable. But with this job, you'll have perks you won't have with any other job working full time."

"Are you doing this because my wife is sister to yours?" Joey told him he was. "I don't need a handout, Joey. We're doing all right."

"No, you're not, and you know it. The two of you are only hours away from losing everything you have. I can and want to help you." It was Mike that asked him what sort of help. "Today, I covered both your mortgages. Not covered, but paid them off. And before you ask, yes, I did that because of Autumn."

Roy burst into tears. As he sat there, sobbing out his pain, Joey looked at Mike. Mike was made of sterner stuff, but he was worried, just as much as Roy was. He didn't know how to be delicate when talking to people. In fact, Joey would say he was terrible with people. But he liked these men and their families and wanted…no, he needed to help them. However he could.

"Mike, you no longer have cancer. Also, you wouldn't have been aware of it, Roy, but you would have been murdered soon. Neither will happen should you both stay here. I want you both to live a very long and happy life. All right?" The man paled, his face as white as the shirt he had on. "I'm not one to mince words. I've been a loner longer than I should have been. I'm not good around people in beating around the bush either. But as of the moment we shook hands, not only was I able to heal you, but I've also made you as immortal as I am. As Autumn and I are."

"I don't know what to say." Joey told him to take the job that would be offered. "I will. Yes, I will. I've not even told June yet. I've been trying to get it right in my head that I'm going to— Thank you seems to be not nearly enough. I'll do whatever you wish of me, Joey. Giving me the opportunity to see my children grow up… well, that's the best a man can hope for."

"It is."

"I don't know how you figured out I was to be murdered, Joey, but I can't thank you enough for telling me. I mean, I'll go wherever you tell me so, like Mike, I can see my children grow up and have kids of their own."

The three of them talked about the upcoming party his family had every year. They'd never attended, as it was just a little too much for them to come that far. The two of them did confess they had cars that were less than what would be considered good. Joey was happy to watch them make fun of each other and their inability to work on even the simplest of things around the house.

"You should have seen me when the dryer broke

down for the umpteenth time. I was working on it, trying not to curse around the children, when I banged up my knuckle so badly I could see bone. Then, rounding them up so I could go and get stitches in it was fun too. I love my children to the ends of the earth, but that day I would have gladly traded them for dogs. By the way, Joey, what are you?"

"Everything. But mostly, I'm a tiger when I need to make a point." The two men said they'd heard that but weren't sure. "My family is as well. Most of the wives of my dad and uncles are as well. My Uncle Evan and his wife, Aunt Dylan, are coming over to have dinner with us. Also, you should be made aware of the fact that Aunt Dylan can be a little bit straight to the point. More so than I am."

"I've seen her around town. I mostly stay out of her way when I can. She's a ball buster, all right. I've never—" One of the children came into the room with them and was polite when he asked him if he could have a snack. "Benji. You don't go asking people you don't know for snacks. My goodness."

"It's all right. I'm your uncle too." Joey told the men he'd be back. "I think we might have just what you're looking for. And after dinner, I know that Mary Margaret is going to have some lovely desserts. What's your favorite?"

"Ice cream. We don't get it very often. It's expensive, and our freezer has a mind of its own, Momma said. But when I get it, I like just plain old white. My brother, he makes fun of me on account of it being just plain white. I think it's the bestest flavor of all." He told the little boy he liked it as well. "I like sherbet too. But it's more than ice cream, so we never have it but for special times. You sure are big, aren't you?"

"I am. All my family is." Joey lifted Benji up on the stool he'd sat on plenty of times when he'd been a child. "Mary Margaret, this young man is going to expire if he doesn't get a snack to have before dinner. What do you have for a growing young boy?"

"Oh, I'm sure we can find him something. I have good snacks and some your momma might frown upon. Which is it going to be, young man?" He said he'd have a good snack and sounded so dejected Joey had to laugh. "Momma said snacking is all right, but we shouldn't spoil our dinner over it."

"I think she's right. But we can sort of mix it up a bit, don't you think, Mary Margaret? A lot of good and a couple of bad for you ones?" She winked at him and told them she had just the ticket. "I love snacking when I can get to it. But usually, I forget to eat, and by the time I realize it's well past mealtime, I have an entire meal."

Benji must have told the other kids where he was headed, and they soon joined them in the kitchen. They all wanted to sit on the other stool, so Joey produced several more for them to sit on. He was sitting with them when the women joined him in the kitchen. Kissing

Autumn on the mouth got just the reaction he'd given his parents when they kissed in front of him. Laughing, he didn't even inquire if it was all right for them to have a nice snack before they had dinner.

"Uncle Joey likes to eat stuff that's good for him. I think he's afraid of his momma." Benji nodded to the little boy speaking. Joey thought his name was Michael and told him he was afraid of his momma. "Will she be my aunt too? I need lots of aunts. My teacher is going to make us an ant farm, and she said we had to be careful with it."

"Not that kind of ant, you dummy. The kind that are outside on the sidewalk." Benji looked at Joey as he continued. "Sometimes these kids get on my last nerve, but I kinda like them."

He'd gotten that from his mother, Joey thought. As they ate their snacks, Autumn told him she'd given her sisters a tour of the house. The fathers joined them just about the time Autumn was explaining to her nephews why they'd never seen her before.

"I've been really busy trying to get my life together. But I'm around now, so we'll be able to have fun together. We have a pool out back too." The boys said they had to have swimming lessons this summer. "That's a good thing to have. I'd be heartbroken if one of you were hurt while here."

Joey watched Autumn with her family. She was a great deal more relaxed than she'd been before. Even when his mom showed up, she told him she noticed it as well. Mom even told him she was looking forward to having little guys around. His family had a great many little girls of late.

Benji looked at his dad like he was sizing him up for something. Joey did wonder what was going to spill from the kid's mouth when he asked his dad if he could talk to him. Man to man, he said. Dad, of course, agreed, and they all waited for him to speak.

"You have any jobs for me, mister?" Dad, ever great around the kids, asked him what he could do. "Nothing much, I guess. Momma said I'm too little to mow yet. And she won't let me drive either. I asked her why, and she said I had to pass a test. I don't know how to read much, so I can't do that. But I can pick up some sticks if you need it." Benji leaned very close to his dad and whispered the rest to him. "We don't got enough money for Peter to pay Paul. I don't know who they are, but I was hoping if I could help my mom and dad, then Peter and Paul will leave us alone. They call the house all the time."

Dad looked at him over Benji's head. Telling his dad through their link that he was helping them out, Dad looked back at the young boy. He could tell he was touched by the boy's need to help his family, so he wasn't surprised when Dad told him if he wanted to do odd jobs for him, he could surely use him. Joey loved his dad, but right at that moment, he thought for sure he could have fallen over and worshipped the man.

Of course, the rest of them wanted a job too. "I have a swing set in my back yard that I was thinking of moving over here for Joey and Autumn to have when they have kids. Will you guys be able to test it out for me? I'd surely hate to have anything happen to someone if it's not all that much fun anymore." Benji looked at his parents before committing to anything. When June nodded at him, Benji looked back at his dad. "In fact, tomorrow I'd like to pick you guys up in my car and bring you over to my home for a few hours. My son, Joey here, he needs to talk to your parents, and that would help him out a great deal to be able to do that. Shadow and I have a lot of things at the house that our grandkids use when they come over. Would that be all right with you guys?"

"I don't know. They can be a handful." September looked at Autumn as she continued. "I don't want to overwhelm anyone. They can be quite rambunctious when they want to be. Especially when all of them are together."

"I'm sure we can handle them. At one time, Shadow and I had five children, all in diapers. It was hard then, but when I look back on it, I think we did pretty good. None of them got a rash, and we all lived to tell about it." June finally relented, and then so did September. "You just leave it to us. We'll be great."

"All right then." The women smiled at his mom.

"Does he do this often? Invite strangers to your home under the age of ten? I would brain Roy if he did that."

"He knows we can handle them. After Joey and Autumn speak to you, I'll take the two men to the plants where I want them to work. There is plenty that needs to be gone over. Also, as a bonus, your insurance will start as soon as today. Other perks are a car, paid time off, as well as other things we'll talk about."

They were overwhelmed—Joey could see that on all the adults' faces. It was all right, he figured. They'd get used to the way his family just barged in and did things. When Dylan and his uncle showed up, they sat down to dinner. And just as he predicted, Dylan was telling them how things were going to go from now on, and they seemed to be taking it well.

Joey took Autumn's hand into his. Kissing the back of it, he could feel her tension. Asking her about it, she told him she would tell him later. It wasn't terrible, she told him, but not wonderful either. Whatever it was, she'd get to the bottom of it, and there wouldn't be any reason for anyone to stress anymore.

Chapter 5

Autumn was just getting ready to leave the house when her cell phone rang. She'd not had it very long, but now that she had it, she couldn't believe she'd gone so long without it. Her two sisters could contact her when they needed something. Even though she could talk to Joey through their link, he would call her sometimes to ask her about this or that. This time it was June.

"I have a question for you. I don't know how you did it, but did you put an ungodly amount of money in our checking account? If so, then you have to go to the bank with me. The bank manager is being a prick about it." She asked June what was going on. "He is claiming we've done something nefarious to get the money and has called the police. Right now, I'm on my way to the bank with two officers with me. I'm just glad Mike isn't here. He'd freak out if he was."

"I'm sorry. I did put the money in your account,

but I don't understand why the manager is all up in arms about it. If he took the time to look at the account, he could see that the money was transferred from my account. I'll meet you there. Is September with you?" She said she had called her first to get Autumn's number. "I'm sorry, June. I should have made sure it was something you knew before this."

"I don't mind. Not at all. Having a plus bank account is something I've not had in a very long time. But I am going to pay you back, Autumn. I don't want money to come between us." Autumn assured her it never would. "I've seen what lending family members money can do to people." Autumn told her not to think of it as a loan then. "You've put a great deal of money in my account, Autumn. About as much as Mike and I make in six months of scraping and going without. I have to pay you back."

She was headed to her car when she answered her sister. "I have a great deal of money, June. More than I can spend in several lifetimes. I'm good at making it, and so is Joey. You take it because I want you to not be stressed out about money. This way, when the kids want something, you don't have to tell them no." June said again it was a lot of money. "It is. And I'm glad you can appreciate that it is. I'm thrilled I could do it. But it's done. Move on. I'm leaving my house now. I'll see you two at the bank."

Driving in, she spoke to Shadow. Telling her

what was going on and asking for advice to deal with it, Shadow told her she was in town and would meet her there. Autumn told her it was all right, but Shadow knew the banker better than she did.

"He's a shithead if you want the truth. I've been dealing with him and his kind all my frigging life. I had the same trouble with him when I got my first commission check. Not the same man, of course, but one like him." Autumn asked her why she was still using the bank if she was having issues with him. "You know what? That's an excellent question. I'm going to make a couple of calls right now. I'm in the parking lot, so I'll be in as soon as I make some calls. Fucker. This will teach him to be a prick."

Autumn was still laughing when she entered the imposing building. There was nothing friendly in the place. Banks of the old days were built to intimidate people, to show off their wealth. This one looked like it wasn't just trying to show off, but like they hadn't paid their electric bill either. It was that dark inside.

Her sisters were sitting on one of the couches just inside the front door. They both stood up when she entered and hugged her. Autumn thought she could get used to this but was stopped from commenting when Mr. Waddell came to talk to them. He did not look like a friendly man to her. In fact, she thought if he were armed, he'd be pointing his gun at the three of them.

"I don't know why they insisted on calling you.

The police are taking care of this matter for me." She asked him what the matter was. "They're trying to tell me the money in the accounts, their accounts, is theirs. I have a right to ask where they got it."

"No, you don't. You have no rights at all. Was there a problem with the money getting into the account? Did anyone tell you not to accept money from them?" He told her it was his duty to make sure the bank wasn't being swindled. "Swindled how? Because if I'm thinking of this in the right way, they put their money into the bank to use. How is that even remotely swindling you out of anything?"

"I will ask the questions here, young lady." Whatever he was going to say, June told her it wasn't worth it. She said they could go to another bank. "You do that. You go on and do that and see what happens when they find out you've gotten this money under suspicious circumstances."

Shadow winked at her as she went to stand in line at the tellers. Mr. Waddell nearly broke his neck trying to get to Shadow to talk to her. Autumn told her sisters to watch this. This was going to be epic.

"Mrs. Whitfield. It's so nice to see you again. How is your family? Is there anything I can help you with?" She shook her head and was called next in line to a teller. When she told the woman she wanted to close her account, Mr. Waddle nearly fell over. "Close your account? Whatever for? Is someone here treating you badly? You just give me the word, and I'll have them fired right now. We are a good bank. If there are any troubles, then I'd like to be the first one to know about it. Don't do that, Shelly. She's going to leave it there. Correct, Mrs. Whitfield?"

"Nope. I've had enough of the bullshit prejudice shit that goes on here. I've already spoken to the rest of my family, and they're going to do the same." She looked at them as Oliver and Eve, Joey's grandparents, came into the bank to close their accounts. "I see they're already moving on it. Good. The sooner, the—"

"Mrs. Whitfield. If you take your money out of this bank, we'll have no way of keeping it open. And if the rest of your family does the same, I'm afraid there is no hope for us at all. You must tell me what the issue is so I can fix it." She told Mr. Waddle it was all him. "Me? I have never said a bad word about you or any of your family. They mean the world to me."

"Do they? Well, my daughter-in-law was trying to help her sisters with some money, and you accused them of a life of crime rather than letting them take some of the money out for personal usage." He looked at her, and Autumn winked at him. She could see he was remembering every word he'd said to them. "You have no idea how embarrassing it was for me to find out not only that you've accused them of terrible things, but you also told them to go to another bank. So we are."

While they were standing there, David and Joshua, uncles of Joey's, came in to close their accounts as well.

The entire town looked like they were coming in too when word got around that the Whitfields were closing their accounts. The police, as well as Joey, showed up a few minutes later to escort Mr. Waddle out of the building. Once he was gone, Shadow turned to Autumn's sisters.

"It should be clear sailing for you now. I don't think you're going to have any trouble with money or the banks again." When Shadow's cell phone rang, her sisters went to the tellers to pull out their money too, only to be told there wasn't enough cash in the place for them as well as the Whitfields. "Hang on a moment, Mr. Price. I have my family here with me now. I have to tell you, this is a terrible way to treat my family. Can you imagine what that monster said to my new family? I was embarrassed. And pissed off."

Shadow put the phone on speaker. "I'm so very sorry about this. The Whitfield family is our bread and butter for this bank, and I thought Henry was aware of it. Even if he didn't know your new family was the ones needing to take some cash out, that was no way to treat our customers. I want to make it up to you all. Please, just let us have a second chance here, and I'll make this right. I promise you, you'll not have any more trouble so long as you're using our banks." She told the bank president she'd have to talk to her family about this, as it had hurt them all to have family treated this way. "I would imagine it has. But as soon as tomorrow morning, I will have a new bank manager in there, and you'll see I take my customer service very seriously. I swear to you, I will fix this."

After ten more minutes of the manager talking to Shadow, they decided to leave the bank as it was. Both June and September took out enough money to pay the schools' fees, as well as to take the children shopping for new coats. Going to lunch with them was a little more crowded than she'd thought it would be, but they did have fun.

"I'd like for you two and your families to move closer to me. I know it's a big move, and I won't blame you if you tell me to fuck off. But having you back in my life has become a priority to me." September told her that she and June were talking about that last night. "Good. Then we can start looking for homes now. I know you need more room, both of you, so we'll start there."

"You're not buying us a house, Autumn." She smiled at them both. "Don't you dare give me that innocent look either. I don't know you as well as I had hoped by this time in my life, but I can buy a home. By the way, what happened to Uncle Ross's house? May told us it was gone, but I went by there on the way here, and it is really gone. It looks as if it's never been there."

Opening her palm, she showed them the tiny version of the house. When they both stared at it, as if they couldn't believe the details, Autumn told them what she'd done. It was funny, the expressions on their faces when she was finished.

"So you just shrunk it down to fit in your pocket? I know you did that, but I'm still having trouble wrapping my head around — I just saw the cat that was forever in the yard. Good lord, you really did shrink it down." Autumn laughed. "You must be a great deal more magical than you let on. Joey told us he was very powerful, but this? Well, I just don't know what to say to it."

Lunch was finished by three o'clock. They'd also talked over a great many things Autumn needed to make them aware of. Not just the money, though they did keep coming back to that one, but also what being immortal meant. Autumn had a feeling they still didn't understand it, but they would eventually.

Once they were finished up with the things she'd had on her list, June asked her if she was going to go and see their parents. She wondered why that would be a question when September spoke too.

"We were thinking it would be wonderful to let them see how successful you've become. And how simply beautiful you are. I know it's sort of mean and petty, but I think…both me and June think it would really piss them off if they were to realize everything they did to you was in vain. That despite them, or perhaps even because of them, you've made yourself a wonderful life." September laughed. "I know you're thinking we've lost our minds. Perhaps we have, but to have them know that not only have you become this very wonderful person, but you've been helping us as well. That will put a stick up their asses."

Autumn smiled and told them she'd think about it. "Thank you. I had hoped you'd not just tell us no." June leaned in to speak quietly when she spoke to her again. "May called me yesterday to tell me I had to take her up to see them. I told her I had my children home and that if I did that, which I wasn't anyway, they'd have to come with me. She hung up on me."

Autumn promised them she really would think on it, but kind of in the back of her mind thought she'd do it, if for no other reason than what they'd said — to be petty and mean to them. They talked about everything under the sun after that, even about how much they were glad she was back in their lives. Autumn was as well. Having family was much better than she'd thought it would be after leaving home.

Later that evening, she was talking to Joey about her day. He said he'd had fun as well. Hanging out with the men was something he'd never done as a younger man. Even Bennett had gone with them. He was the one that had hired Mike. Mike, apparently, had the best understanding of ordering and running a distribution center's trucks coming and going that Bennett had ever seen. He'd been hired on the spot.

"Roy is going to be working with my mom on three projects. I guess he's also a computer person and can make out spreadsheets like she needs. They'll track the flow of money sent each month to keep three of her businesses running, and Roy said he could do that. Mom is thrilled beyond words." Autumn asked him if he thought they'd like living so close to them. "Roy told me if he could have, he'd have moved them here the first time he met us. Mike was a little more cautious about it. I think he's sending money, money they don't really have, to keep his mom in the nursing home. I had Mom look to see if she was getting good care. She's going to get back with me."

"Good. I've never met her, but then that's not hard to believe." She leaned back on the couch and closed her eyes for a moment. "Your mom is scary as fuck. You know that?"

"I do know that. And when she's all hyped up about some wrongdoing, she can be an absolute monster. Dad just lets her take care of things like that." Autumn told him she wanted to be just like her. "Honey, I don't know if you know this or not, but you are just like her. A little scarier since you have all that magic. To be honest, I think she's a little in awe of you too."

Good, she thought. It was nice to have someone liking her. Autumn made a list of shit she had to get done in the morning and went up to bed when Joey did. The day after tomorrow was going to be a big day. She'd decided to go and see her parents.

~~~

May felt her face be all smiles today. She was there seeing her mom and dad. It had taken a great deal to get January to drive her up here, but it was well worth having to put up with her bitching and moaning about the cost. She didn't even pay for her gas—why did it bother her so much?

"No. I'm not going to think of that. Not now." She was speaking out loud again, something she'd only just caught herself doing. When she was younger, that's all she'd done—talk through things until she had it right. Then people began to talk about her being crazy. May stopped that shit. Both the talking about her and talking out loud.

Even though January had brought her up here, she decided she was much too tired to go and see her parents. May didn't understand her sisters at all. She'd be here daily if she could make it. As it was now, without a car or any money, she was lucky she'd gotten herself a hotel room. Cheap, yes, but at least she was no longer sleeping in boxes. May shivered when she thought of the one and only time she'd had to do that.

Harvey had not only given her cash—not nearly as much as she wanted or needed—but he'd also given her two weeks in a hotel. That wasn't what she was used to either, but it was all he'd do. Since she'd planned to outlive the bastard or kill him off, she'd gone ahead and signed the prenup he'd put in front of her, knowing if she failed at her plans, she'd be devastated. And now here she was, in her forties, no money, no home, and no one to bitch at.

When her dad sat down in front of her, she was giddy with excitement. Her daddy was near, and she'd tell him everything before moving on to her mommy. May knew she was too old to be calling them that, but that was what she'd always called them, and now she was older, it was still a comfort for her to call them that.

"Did you forget something, Daughter?" He'd always call her that when she'd upset him in any way. Of course, that was the extent of his being upset with her. After she felt shamed, he'd find Autumn and take his anger at whatever she'd done out on her. "I didn't get my usual package from you. Why not? Did you want to give it to me personally? Is that it?"

"My husband has filed for divorce. I don't have a place to live, and he cut me off. The things I brought you were expensive, Daddy. I don't even have a credit card." He just stared at her, another thing he did when he was upset with her. "I've had such a time of it. Autumn is causing us trouble again. Out there—"

"So, what you're telling me is you didn't think of your father and how bad he has it." She said she was basically homeless. "And I'm in prison, Daughter."

The hardness of the way he said it this time hurt her all the way to her feet. He didn't speak to her for several minutes, and she had the need to explain herself— something May Sheffield rarely did.

"Daddy, I didn't have the funds to even come up here to see you. I had to beg January to bring me here.

She's out in the car. I'm the one that comes to see you. I'm in a hard place right now, and—"

"Yes, I can see where you'd think you have it so much worse than I do. While you're out there riding in cars, having lunch with your friends, I'm in here. In prison. Where I don't get to order my food. I wear what they tell me." He huffed at her. "Did you or did you not bring me anything to stave away the time while I'm here? In prison."

"No." When he turned to the guard that had brought him here, Daddy told him he was ready to go back to his cell. "Daddy, please. I'll make it up to you. I promise you. I'll bring you double the next time."

"Don't bother trying to suck up to me." He paused while he was being taken back. "Perhaps I'll have someone call Autumn. I'm betting she'd be able to provide me with just a little happiness. Unlike you have. Goodbye, Daughter. Don't bother coming back here until you remember who brought you into this world and how much you owe me."

Then, he was gone.

"May? What is wrong with you?" She looked at her mommy and started to cry. "Goodness, don't do that. Do you want the others to think you're an idiot? Straighten up your shit or go home. I don't have time for you to be sobbing all over me."

"Daddy left me without me being able to talk to him." She asked her what she'd done to him. That her daddy was the best man in the world. "He's upset with me because I didn't bring him anything. I tried to tell him I was getting a divorce, but he—"

"I suppose that means you've not brought me those chocolates, have you?" She told her they were expensive. She'd paid fifty dollars a pound to have them imported for her. "Like I care how much they cost. You didn't bring them. Is that what you're telling me? That I'm to do without because you have a husband that kicked you to the curb? I told you, May, time and time again, that you're better off just robbing a bank than getting married."

"I don't remember you ever telling me that." Mother, like Daddy, had huffed at her. "I'm living in a hotel for the next few weeks, then I'm homeless. Autumn did something with Uncle Ross's home, and now I can't stay there."

"Homeless? Well, doesn't life just suck for you? Poor baby. My daughter is homeless and has no money." May had needed just this from her parents. At least her mom was on board. "I'm in prison, and I'm never going to get out. There you are in a hotel, where they make the beds for you. Clean up after you. While I have to make my own bed and take a shower with other women. No pretty soaps left in my bathroom. No sirree. I'm stuck in here while my ungrateful daughter can't even save enough money up to buy her mother, who is in prison, a box of chocolates. I guess I can see where you think you have it so bad."

"Mommy, that's not fair." Mom stood up but sat down quickly when she was told by her guard. "You have a roof over your head. Meals three times a day that I don't have."

"I'd like to go back to my cell, please." When she was taken to the door, she said nearly the same thing her daddy had said to her. "I should get in contact with Autumn. I am her mother, after all. Perhaps now that she's married to the richest family in the entire world, she'll be able to bring me something when I ask for it."

Sitting there long after they left her, she tried to think how this had gone all wrong. They were going to call Autumn? Make her their favorite daughter? That wasn't going to happen. She wasn't going to allow anyone to usurp her place with her family. Pulling out her phone, she remembered she couldn't make any kind of Internet connection in here and moved to leave. She had to be stopped to sign out when her mind was on other things.

"How did it go?" She looked at January and asked her what she'd said to her. "I was asking how it went. I thought you'd be in there a lot longer. Good thing I didn't go into town to get something to do. Remember, you owe me lunch anyway."

"Yes. I forgot. It went very well. Mommy and Daddy were both disappointed you didn't make it in to see them. Mommy was particularly upset about it, but I was able to calm the waters for you. You should make an effort, January. They are our parents." They were going to call Autumn? That kept circling around and around in her mind until she was sick with it. "Pull over. I'm going to be sick."

Even as the car was rolling to a stop, May leaned out of her open door and puked. There was blood in her vomit, just like there had been yesterday when she'd eaten something at the hotel that hadn't agreed with her. Getting out, staggering to the side of the road, she sat there with her head down between her legs and prayed not to be sick again.

"Christ, May. Are you all right? There's blood in your puke. What on earth is wrong with you?" She didn't know and said that to her sister. "You'd better get that checked out. That is some serious blood loss you have going on there. Did you eat something?"

"I'm not sure what I did. Yesterday I had a nice meal at the hotel, and that made me sick too." January asked her why she was eating in a hotel. "Harvey is filing for divorce. At least he says he is. The man can't do anything without me right there to tell him how to do it."

"That sucks. Sorry to hear that. But you have to get this checked out. Have you eaten anything since you were sick yesterday?" She'd only been able to hold down sips of water but told her sister she had been eating just fine. It was stress. "I can see that. But still. You need to make sure it's nothing else. You do remember how Uncle Ross died, don't you?"

She had no idea. He wasn't anyone she ever gave a thought to other than how he'd left all his worldly goods to Autumn. There she was again. Autumn. May had to do something before the bitch took over everything she had lined up for herself.

"Do you suppose you could take me to the emergency room? You don't have to stay, January. I know you're very busy. Just drop me off at the entrance, and I'll go it alone." January fell for her pitiful comments just as she thought she would. Not only did she say she'd stay with her, but she'd call the others too. "Thank you so much. I'm afraid, January.

She was too, but not about being sick. It was that Autumn was going to be her parents' favorite girl. Well, not so long as she had breath in her body, she'd not be. Autumn needed to see the light. And May was just the person to show her.

Getting back into the car with the help of her sister, May leaned back in the car seat and closed her eyes. She wasn't thinking about anything but Autumn and how to teach the bitch a lesson. By the time they arrived at the emergency room, May was feeling a little worse. She knew it was going to be nothing but stress. And that was Autumn's fault as well.

Chapter 6

Now that she was here, Autumn wished she'd thought this through a little better. Seeing her parents wasn't something she should be putting herself through. However, since she'd spoken to June earlier this morning, she knew it had to be done. The things her father had said to her had been horrific.

"He called me last night. Dad said I was to kill May and that she's no longer a part of our family. Like I could do that." Autumn asked her if he'd given her a reason. "Yes. He told me she'd neglected her duties as his daughter and left them, I guess he meant him and Mom, hanging dry. He also told me that even you would have known better than to come empty handed to see them. He told me he was in prison like ten times like I hadn't any idea where he might be. I don't want to do this. I'm not going to do this."

"Of course you're not. Let me think a moment."

Reaching out to her father, she read his mind and his anger at May. The reason was too ludicrous to believe, so she checked out her mother. Yes, they were both upset because May hadn't brought them anything in the way of snacks and money. "You said they wanted you to kill May. Would you like to know why they want you to do that?"

"I don't know. Do I?" Autumn had laughed then. And when June did, she felt better. "Tell me. I might well not believe it either, but tell me, so I'm armed with information if they call back asking me why she's still up and walking around."

After explaining to June what had upset them and that they'd shoved Autumn in May's face, June was as shocked as she'd been. June sputtered around for a second before she finally spoke where she could understand her.

"Chocolate. They want me to kill May because she didn't bring them chocolate? That's the most...well, I was going to say the stupidest reason I've ever heard to want someone dead, but it's not. The three of them deserve each other." They both laughed again. "I'm so sick of them. I wish May would get her head out of her ass and realize they're playing her. She's always thought of herself as their preferred daughter. I think they had all of us thinking the same thing for a while. You would have thought she'd have outgrown this sort of petty stuff. But not May. She's still calling them Mommy and Daddy. Like she's a five year old."

Now, here she was, waiting on her parents to talk to her. With a few strings pulled from Dylan, they were both going to see her at one time, and they had a private room in which to do it in. Once they were brought in, she wasn't going to give them an opportunity to speak, just blast them and leave.

Her father came in first. She'd not seen him in at least a decade, and he looked like he'd aged several hundred years. When her mother was brought in, Autumn thought she looked worse than her father. Both of them stared at her as if they had no idea who she was. It occurred to her that they might well not.

"It's Autumn Whitfield. Your youngest." Father said he knew that. Mother just huffed. "You've been making phone calls that are going to stop. Today. I've made it so you are no longer allowed to make calls."

"You can't do that." She just stared at her mother. "I need to call people. It's the only pleasure I have since you made us have to go to prison."

"*I* made you go? I think it was you that mixed up the poison you fed me. The two of you poured it down my throat. You're here for all sorts of things you did to me." Mother huffed. "I'm not here to debate why you're here. I'm just glad you are. June told me you wanted her to kill May. That's not going to happen either. Stop pitting them against each other before that turns out badly."

"Are you threatening us?" She said she was merely making them see reason. At least she was trying to do that. Her mother huffed again. "We should have tried harder to smother you when you were a baby. Not that we didn't try, I'll tell you that. But that fucking magic you didn't share kept you from being dead. Did you know that when someone put a pillow over your face, even as a week old baby, the pillow would burst into flames? It didn't burn you either. Just gutted out, and you'd laugh. Like killing you was a game. Fucking bitch."

Autumn hadn't considered sitting down at the table with them. But when her mother said that to her, her knees simply gave out. Asking her why they'd hated her so much got her nothing but more huffs. More glares. Finally, when she thought she could stand again without falling on her ass, she stood up.

"As of the moment I leave here, the two of you will no longer be able to have visitors unless I approve them. Also, before I forget to ask you. Were you aware that both your conversations as well as phone calls are recorded and transcribed to a computer? They know you told June to kill May. Also, what you've said in here." Mother asked her why they'd care. They were just talking. "Sure you are. And you didn't threaten to call me over May when you wanted to hurt her. I wouldn't bring you chocolates unless it was to make smores at your funeral. Also, there will be no money put into your account anymore. I was doing that, not May. She might well have taken credit for it, but it was me, trying to make your lives a little better."

"What do you mean, you won't be putting money

in our accounts? I'm your father, and what I say goes. You will do that. You owe us for having us put in here in the first place." Father glanced at her mother, then back at her with a glare. "What sort of daughter puts her dear parents in prison? Then when they're down and out, she takes the one joy from them that they have. You're despicable, Autumn. I'm ashamed to even think of you as our daughter."

"That won't work on me. I could care less if you're hurt and going without. I should have done this a long time ago. As a prisoner, you don't deserve anything nice as far as I'm concerned." She laughed then. "To think that for some reason, I thought you'd be happy I'd been taking care you had extras and that you'd like me a little. But you never will, will you? I'm just wondering what it was about me that made you hate me so much."

"You know." But she didn't and told her mother that. "You were nothing like the others. Always wanting to do the right thing. Christ, it was an embarrassment for us to even tell our friends you were our daughter. The fact you couldn't hold out for just a few more hours to be born really fucked things up for us too."

"You mean because you couldn't call me October? That's what has pissed you off? You know you could have still called me that. No one would have cared." Mother told her they were going to have an entire set of monthly babies, but she had fucked that up too. "So all this time, it's not because I had the magic that was handed down to me. It wasn't because I was the youngest. It was simply because I was born one day early and screwed up your babies. Christ, that is about the stupidest thing you've ever said to me. And let me tell you, you've said some really dumbass things over my lifetime."

"Why are you here? We didn't send for you. Go away." Dylan spoke in her ear while her mother was going on about how she was ungrateful and that they didn't want her coming around anymore. She had to sit down again, but this time it was because of what she'd been told by Dylan.

"I just heard that May is ill. That she has stage-four cancer throughout her body. They only give her a few months to live." Neither of them said a word, but she could tell by the expressions on their faces that they were confused. "Did you hear what I said? May is dying. She doesn't have much time left."

"So? What do you expect us to do about it? It's not like, even if we were out of here, that we'd run to her aid. Whatever gave it to her, it's nothing to do with us." Father nodded as if he'd come to a decision. "I want you to talk to January. Tell her she must take over for May and her duties to us. I'd not want anything from you if you were the last person on this earth. The money, yes, we'll still get the money monthly. That goes without saying. Make sure you put a little extra in there for us too. Things are going up, you know."

There was so much she could say to them. So much

she could do too. But she only told the guard she was ready to leave, and she opened the door for her. Autumn was sitting at one of the picnic tables when Dylan spoke to her again. But first, she asked if she was all right.

I'm not sure. I told my parents what you told me, and they were more concerned about what this was going to do to them rather than anything May might have going on with her. Dylan asked her how she was doing again. *I have no idea how I'm supposed to feel right now. I'm not really surprised, but then again, I am. I don't think I've ever had their selfishness slammed into my face like this before. They're nothing to me. I mean, who says those sorts of things about their own children? Don't answer that. I know. Them.*

Sometimes the best is brought out in parents when they're in prison. Sometimes. However, in this case, I think it's only made them more terrible people.

Autumn said she was leaving there now. Dylan told her she'd meet her in town.

I can do that. But I didn't drive here. If you tell me when you get to the restaurant, I'll just be there.

Oh. You're doing your witchy stuff, are you? All right. I'm close to the restaurant now. When I park, I'll let you know. Christ, to have had that sort of thing when I was out in the field would have been amazing. But you're wonderful for doing shit for us when we need it too. Autumn laughed. Leave it to one of Joey's aunts to put things in perspective for her. *I nearly forgot to tell you. Your sister June has found a house she loves. The bank, however, isn't going to be able to lend her the money because of her past record in being behind. I think she was pretty devastated.*

She was or still is devastated? Dylan told her she was. *So how much do I owe you for buying the house? I'm sure it wasn't cheap.*

Believe it or not, it was one we already owned. It was a rental for a long time, then recently we've had it renovated to charge more rent. Having her and her family own it has saved us a lot of time and effort in keeping the renters out of our hair. I'm doing the same for September. There are several more houses the family owns that she could pick from to take off our hands. Autumn asked her if her sisters knew the houses were theirs now. *I don't think we got around to discussing it. They were just thrilled to be able to feel like they were going to be renting it from us. I didn't go into anything else. I was going to leave that to you.*

Of course, you were. Dylan laughed and said she was at the restaurant now. Popping into her car with her had the other woman screaming, but Autumn laughing. It was great to get one over on them once in a while. "Now that was worth it. Is anyone else joining us for lunch?"

"You scared the fucking shit out of me." Dylan laughed. "I'll get you back for this. See if I don't. And when I do, I'm going to laugh my ass off. In answer to your question, yes, your sisters. Be surprised when they tell you about the houses. And make sure you don't mention the rent thing. I want this to be a good lunch, not a Debby Downer one."

"You're in a mood." They got out of the car, and it hit Autumn right then that Dylan, with all her beauty and wonderful skin, was way older than she was. Christ, she didn't want to think about how much older she was than her. She decided to think about something else. "Do you suppose that someday I'll look back on this thing with my parents and wonder why I was so upset about it? I mean, I'm not really upset, but just amazed someone hasn't killed them before now."

"I don't know. I suppose you could. After a while, things like grudges and people dying around you isn't something you think about. I've been working with presidents for decades, and I don't think about them as being long ago turned to dust. You won't either. You have a practical mind, as I do. They'll come to be just another bump in the road that barely makes you realize they were even there." They entered the restaurant, and she saw her sisters. "I'm glad they'll be around for you and us. I love the two of them as much as I do you. Not so much the others."

"I never thought about that. Will they be immortal as well? To be honest with you, Dylan, I don't want to have them breathing down my neck for the rest of our long lives." Dylan told her she'd have to simply not tell them they were, and they'd not be. "That's it? I just don't put it out there that they could be, and they won't be?"

"Pretty much. You could, I guess, tell them they're not, but why get into that with them? They'll just find some other way of pissing you off." When they were seated, not only did Sunny join them, but the rest of the aunts as well. Even Eve, Joey's grandma, came in to eat with them. "I thought this would be a good time to go over things with you and your sisters. Questions you might have as well as things you've had on your mind about living for a long time."

The room they were in was private. A long buffet was brought in for them that had all kinds of delectable things on it, from sushi to fresh salads. There were different kinds of meat, like fried chicken to gyro meat, to make into a nice soft sandwich. Her sisters tried everything. It was fun, she thought, to be able to spend time like this with them. With all of them. Autumn had never had a great many friends, but she knew that on any level she wanted to think about it, these people would be her friends forever. It was a nice thought to have someone in your corner even when you didn't think you needed anyone else.

"I need to talk to you guys." The others were up to the buffet when she cornered her sisters. "June, the house you're going to be living in, it's paid for. You don't have to make any kinds of payments. No rent, and you can do with it as you wish. It's going to be in your name as soon as Dylan gets the paperwork filed. Okay? And if you take one of the other houses they own, September, you'll have the same thing. A good home close to me."

"No. I don't want you to pay for us a place to live."

Autumn explained to them what Dylan had told her. That the houses were rentals for a long time, and they created more issues than they wanted to deal with as landlords. June looked at September and smiled when she looked at her. "All right then. I'll take it. You'll have to look into the house right next door to me, September. It's within walking distance to me and to Autumn."

They were plotting when she went to get something to drink. Sisters. It was like they'd never had a bad thing happen between them. Now they were going to be within walking distance of not only each other but her as well. Autumn was excited as hell about that.

~~~

Joey looked over the contract that had been given to him. There were a couple of places he thought his dad could do better on, but he knew his dad would want things to come out better for the other side rather than him getting the better deal. He was on the last page of it when Bennett joined him at the table.

Long ago, his uncles and dad had decided they no longer wanted an office at their homes. Dylan still worked from home, simply because she needed a secure network and being out and about wouldn't give her that. But the rest of them had moved all traces of work from home to this centralized office. It housed different areas of their business dealings, and he and Bennett mostly worked from the contracts area. When Joey was home, that is.

"I have something I want you to look at for me. Not so much look at, but to tell me its origins. I have a feeling I know, but right now, it's better to be safe than sorry." Joey looked at the blue velvet bag that was now on the table. "I'm hoping it's not from a robbery that happened several years ago and is indeed a fake I've paid very little money for. I'm really hoping I've not found something no one else has been able to find."

"Why do you care? What I mean is, what does it matter if it's from a robbery? I know you well enough to know you'd turn it in if that's where it came from." Bennett told him he was unable to do that. "Turn it in? Why not? There is something you're not telling me. If you want me to look at this, you have to tell me what the story behind it is."

"It's not a modern time robbery I'm talking about. It's hundreds of years ago." Now Joey's fingers were itching to see what mysteries his brother had brought to him. "It didn't get much time in the news simply because it wasn't something the banking industry wanted out there. That they'd been robbed by an unknown, who had taken them for a great deal of money. There were jewels and gems in this robbery that were, for the most part, returned. However, a necklace said to be worth fifty-eight million was never found."

"You think you have it." Even though it wasn't a question, Bennett nodded. "Is this going to come back and bite us in the ass? I'm not going to be taking part in something nefarious, am I? I know you well enough to know you'd not do that, but this other person — what do you know about them?"

"Nothing. I didn't find it from a person. It was at a garage sale, just sitting on the table like it was nothing more than a bauble. It could still be, but I looked it up. This necklace looks exactly like the one that was never returned." He wanted to ask him why he was hitting garage sales but didn't. He remembered Bennett was forever finding small things at them and selling them for much more. "Will you tell me what it is, Joey? Pretty please?"

They were both laughing when Grandda Oliver joined them. He'd been with Bennett when he found the necklace. Grandda Oliver was rubbing his hands together like this was going to be the find of all time. Joey had his brother dump the contents into his hand instead of him doing it himself.

Joey's plan had been to tease his brother about the piece. To tell him some kind of outlandish story about it that would have him laughing. Instead, the piece seemed to pull at him, not just physically but mentally as well. It took Autumn popping into the room to make him realize he couldn't put the piece down.

"It's cursed." The necklace disappeared out of his hand and landed on the table some feet away from him. Joey was left breathless and his heart pounding. "Joey? Can you hear me? Joey, don't make me have to hit you.

Answer me."

"I'm all right." He was too, but he was no less drained from the piece. "It's like it was sucking me into it. That no matter what I did, I not only needed to own the piece, but I had to kill anyone and everyone that would try and take it from me. Bennett, that wasn't funny if this was a joke."

"I didn't do anything to you. Or to the necklace. I swear it." He apologized twice more before he spoke to him again. "It didn't do anything like that to either Grandda Oliver or I. You should have seen your face, Joey. It was like you were being pulled through a wormhole or something. I couldn't move either. Like it was holding me back from helping you. Grandda, did you feel anything?"

They all looked at Autumn. "I didn't do it." She sounded so much like a child that had been caught that it made him laugh. He even felt better for it. "However, whoever did put the curse on that sucker is long dead. Even before I realized it was harming Joey, I knew it was something evil. Created for and then given to someone to kill them for the maker."

"Why me? I mean, you heard them—they didn't have any reactions to it at all." Autumn looked at him, and he had a feeling he didn't want to know what else she knew about the necklace. "I'm not going to like the answer, am I?"

"Someone in your family had this at one time.

They were the bearer of the necklace to the sorceress to put the curse on it. Then, when no one else had had any issues with it, before and after her husband was gone, she could easily explain away his disappearance, and no one would question her." Grandpa Oliver asked if she'd been able to kill off her husband. "He's not dead. He's a part of the necklace. Even as we stand here talking about him, he is aware of all of us."

"No shit." Autumn laughed and told Bennett it wasn't a fabrication. "I believe you. So, how do we— Do we want to get him out of there? I mean, I haven't any idea how old he might be right now, but he is a relative of Joey's. The first one we've encountered since we were adopted, but we don't know what sort of person he is. For all we know about the man, there could be a very good reason why he was put in the necklace. He might even be some sort of child molester." The necklace moved, jumping up off the table he was sitting at like he was offended somehow. Joey asked his brother to not upset the necklace. "I do believe that's the strangest thing anyone has ever asked me to do."

"What do you want to do?" Joey asked Autumn if she thought she could touch it. "Yes. It's only for your lineage. I have no link to you other than now. And since we have no children, nor am I expecting, then I think I can touch it. Why? What's your plan?"

"No plan, really. But if you can somehow speak to the man, then we can find out what he wants to do. Then after we figure that out, Bennett and Grandda Oliver can decide what they want to do with it." Grandda asked if she could figure out the curse. "Good idea. Maybe the man can't leave the necklace. Is he in the clear piece there or the entire necklace? These are things that can help you guys decide what you want to do."

"It's a diamond, and he's a part of that. He can speak to us, but right now, all he's saying is that he would never molest a child." They all turned to Bennett. "Before we can proceed, you're going to have to tell him how sorry you are."

"Are you fucking with me right now?" Grandda hit Bennett on the back of the head. Joey had been hit like that before. It was more painful than he realized. "Grandda Oliver. They want me to apologize to an inanimate object. You don't think that's a tad weird?"

"Were you not just sitting here with me when it tried to suck your brother into it? Did you miss the part where Autumn told us there was a man inside of this thing? Or perhaps you didn't notice that when you accused it of being a child molester, it jumped up off the table." He was popped in the back of the head a second time. "Tell him you're sorry. Do it, Bennett Whitfield, or I'm going to never go treasure hunting with you again."

"I'm so very sorry." Bennett asked if they thought that was good enough. Both he and Autumn said no. "Why do I have the feeling this is one big joke you're having with me? I've been around you both enough lately to know you can make things jump and move. Tell me if that's what you're doing, and I'll not play tricks on you again."

"While that would be worth it, I swear to you, on my honor of being your brother, that I'm not doing anything but hoping this sucker isn't going to cause us a great deal of trouble. And that, if you ever get to sell this thing, you share with your little brother what you get out of that diamond." None of them needed the money, but it was fun to joke and tease his brother. Joey was younger than Bennett, but not by much. "Also, you have to do this if for no other reason than we'll all wonder."

"True." Bennett looked at the necklace. After a few seconds, he picked it up. Talking directly to it, he did tell it that he was sorry. "You'd not believe how much that very thing goes on nowadays. I'm profoundly sorry that I insulted you. Truly I am."

After he was finished, Autumn put the necklace in her hand. She told them everything she felt from it, even what the man, Patrick James, Earl of White Cottage, was telling her. Apparently, he'd been in the necklace since the late sixteenth century.

"He's not blaming his wife for his demise, but he does wish to be taken out of the diamond. There are things he would like to finish up, and he cannot while trapped inside of her beautiful necklace." Joey asked if she believed him, careful to use their link rather than let the man hear him. She shook her head as she continued.

Autumn told them what she was feeling when he asked her. "He's lying to me. I can tell that much. He was a womanizer, and he had raped most of the staff that was working in the house. He might not be a child molester, but it's not for lack of trying. The man's wife, the one that put him in here, was only fifteen when he wed her. Her parents were supposed to have been taken care of after the wedding, but he didn't hold to his promises. Patrick, of all the people I know, deserves whatever was done to him. Oh, the curse. If he can find someone of his line to take his place, the curse will be broken, and he'll be free. Over my dead body."

She put the necklace on the floor and pointed at it. Magic exuded from her fingertips. Saying a couple of lines of magic he'd not heard before, the diamond lifted from the chain that held it in place. Once it was about four feet off the floor, Autumn snapped her fingers, and Patrick James, Earl of White Cottage, was suddenly in the office with them.

The man standing there before them looked just like he'd think a wealthy lord would look during that time frame. His clothing was ornate. A beard and his hair were neatly trimmed but gray. The coat and hat he wore matched the rest of the clothing he had on like a tailor had gone to great links to make sure he was a fashion plate. The fur and feathers seemed to scream feminine attire. Not to mention his shoes. They were as over the top as the rest of his clothing—big bows and velvet. Joey

wondered what he'd say if they were to put him in a pair
of jeans and a sweatshirt. However, before any of them
could talk to the man, he crumbled to the floor in a pile
of dust and clothing.

"He's gone." Autumn nodded, then looked at
him while Bennett went on about how they'd not gotten
to speak to him. "These clothes alone would be worth
a fortune. Better yet, I'm betting some museum would
love to have them. I think that's what we should do with
them, don't you, Grandda Oliver?"

"Once he was wed to the child, he had her parents
murdered. Unbeknownst to the young woman at the
time of their engagement, she was also going to be used
as a pawn in his treachery to gain more land and the
king's good graces. She would have been used as most
men would have used her back in that time." Joey asked
how she'd found out. "Her maid. She told her she could
help her, and she did. The two of them reigned for a long
time after he disappeared. He also hated that she placed
him in a box and left him there. Until she had something
to show him. Like his son being born. The man was going
to exact revenge on her by ending your life. You are the
last child of his lineage, and he wishes the family to end."

"Thank you." She told him she loved him. "And I
love you so very much. I don't know what Bennett wants
to do with this stone, but you can bet he's going to make
a fortune from it."

"It's yours. It's your birthright." He said to him it

was tainted by the blood of his ancestors, and he wanted nothing to do with it. "I thought that is what you'd say. I'll just put it someplace and let Bennett decide what they're going to do with it. I love you, Joey Whitfield. Very much."

When the diamond disappeared, he pulled Autumn into his arms and held her. He'd been so lucky, he thought, in what transpired here today. Had she not come and saved him from himself, he would have been stuck in that thing for who knew how long before she found him again. Joey was more than lucky, he thought — he was in love with the only person in the world he knew would have his back.

Joey took the contracts he'd been working on for his dad and told him what he'd found in them. Uncle Evan was there, as well as Uncle Adam. After they invited him to have dinner with them, he told them he had his own sort of date. That he was going to celebrate life with his wife. His uncles teased him, but his dad just patted him on the back.

Joey went back to his father after going to the door. Pulling him into his embrace, he told his dad how much he loved him and respected him for raising him to be a good solid individual. And that he was proud to be his son. Then he told him he loved him. More than any son could have loved a father.

Chapter 7

Autumn had a lot of things to do this morning. She only hoped once she got a start on them, she'd be able to feel less stressed about the list she had going. The first thing she had to do was head to the bank so she could combine her accounts with Joey's. He'd already done his part, and all she needed to do was go in, sign the paperwork, and be done with it. Then there were the credit cards they both had that she was going to have destroyed and closed out.

She was also determined not to have lunch with the women again. Autumn loved spending time with them — a big change for her — but they really could take a lunch hour and stretch it out to be several hours. It was fun but time consuming. Also, now that her sisters were both settled, she could visit them whenever she wanted, so that too was going to be wonderful.

Looking down at her list, she decided if she walked

to town—not far, really, but about a mile—she could get more work done. Driving would entail her having to find a parking spot, then remembering where she'd parked the sucker. She had to admit, however, having a little car all of her own was very nice.

Can I add one more thing to your list? She growled at Joey, and he laughed. *If you knew how incredibly sexy I found that you'd never do it again. Which would be very sad. But seriously, we need some things we didn't get when we went shopping. It's just a few things, I swear.*

Do you have any idea how long my list is of things we didn't get while shopping? A few things is turning into a nightmare. Laughing, she wrote down what he'd told her. *Not too bad. I have most of that on my list already. How are the meetings going?*

Slow. I don't blame my uncles for wanting everyone in on this stuff, but it could have been done in a letter, I think. But then, I'm not too keen on being in a room with fifty people I barely know. Dad wants me to take over a few jobs he's been doing for his dad. She asked him if that was a good thing. *It is. I've been avoiding working with the family for obvious reasons. It's time I get my foot in the door.*

I'm glad you're in agreement. Shadow has asked me to take over one or two of her projects as well. She's giving me a few weeks to get things squared away between the two of us. I wasn't really sure what she meant by that. He told her. *Oh. I guess I didn't think of May as being something that needs squared away. I doubt they even let her out of the hospital yet.*

I don't know. The last time I spoke to Aunt Dylan, she said she's already in the final stages of it. That sucks for her. I've seen people that are where she is. You, as a matter of fact. Autumn didn't want to think about that, so she asked Joey to change the subject. *Gladly. Aurora wants me to talk to her later this afternoon. She knows I've been tweaking areas around the world that needed just a little extra. I don't know what she'll want, but would you like to go with me?*

It depends on how many more little things you add to my day. They both laughed. *I need to get going. I seriously have too much on my plate at the moment. Before I forget to tell you, there is a large envelope for you on the dining room table. It doesn't have a return address on it, but it has your name on it.*

He said he'd look at it as soon as he got home. *Have fun, and if I think of anything else, I'll give you a call. I love you, Autumn.* She told him she loved him as well. *Be safe.*

"Always."

Just as the connection closed, she heard something from the kitchen. She knew Mary Margaret was making pies today with the berries she'd gotten yesterday and wondered what had happened.

When she was about to enter the room, she heard the doorbell. "I have it."

Opening the front door, she was dismayed to find no one there. Autumn called out for the person who might be around, but since there was no car, nor was there anything on the stoop, she made her way back into the house. Autumn was gathering up her purse and things when Mary Margaret called for her.

"I thought I heard you calling for me. Did you need for me—?"

The pain to the back of her head had her falling forward. Even as she fell to the floor, Autumn was sick with the pain. She couldn't breathe or think beyond it. Covering her head with her hands the best she could, Autumn just knew from how badly she was being beaten that it was one of her sisters. Then she let the darkness take her.

~~~

Joey was making notes on the things being said. He could recall most anything, but he thought Dad would trust that he was paying attention more if he was—

The pain had him pitching forward. Knocking over two of the people just in front of him, he cried out as he felt his ribs break under some unseen hand. Screaming for someone to help him, Joey blacked out. When he came around again, he knew it had only been a couple of seconds. He looked into the worried face of his father.

"Someone hit me." Dad told him no one had. "I felt it, Dad. It was like— Autumn. She needs me right now."

Standing up, he was dizzy. The pain was going away, but he could still feel each of the blows that broke more bones. Centering his mind on the pain to make it fade more, he reached for Autumn, only to hit a blank space, like she was no longer there. Dropping to his knees, he told his dad that she was gone.

"No. Son, listen to me. She's unconscious. Autumn is immortal, just as you are. But you need to get to her. I'm calling the police now. Do you know if she's still home?" He said they'd just spoken a moment ago, and she'd been there. "Good. Yes, don't drive, but just get to her."

"I am. I'm going to use my magic." Dad nodded, but the look on his face still worried Joey in ways he'd not felt before. "Come to the house."

I'm going to leave here now, Joey. Keep telling me what you're seeing. All right?

As soon as he was in the house, the kitchen, he could smell fresh blood. Rounding the big table that Mary Margaret had wanted, he found her body. Touching his fingers to her throat, his hand came away with blood. Her throat had been sliced open. Joey told his dad, who was talking to Aunt Dylan.

Mary Margaret has had her throat slit. She's dead. I don't see where there was a fight, so whoever did this must have caught her off guard. I'm going to look for Autumn. He hurt for Mary Margaret's family. She was such a wonderful person, it pissed him off that she'd died like this.

The dining room was empty. There was a noise coming from the living room, and he went there by way of the hall. As soon as he saw May standing over Autumn, a bat in her hands, he put his hands on her neck and snapped it. She fell in Autumn's blood, which was all over the floor as well as on the walls around her.

I've killed May, Dad. Dad sobbed. He asked him twice if he'd found Autumn. *Yes. She's been beaten badly. I have to save her.*

Don't. He asked his father why not while touching his fingers to her shoulder, where it was already turning a dark blue. *You can't give her anything, Joey. No blood or any magic. The police will need to follow this by the books. So will you. I can't imagine you there with her and not being able to help her, but keep telling yourself she's immortal. Please, son. Don't do anything that will jeopardize your getting out of jail for killing May.*

I'm going to be arrested. Dad told him he more than likely would be, but to cooperate with everyone. *Will you come with me, Dad? I don't know that I can do this alone. Please? And will you have Mom go to the hospital with Autumn? To keep us informed of what is going on there.*

Yes. I'll tell her. Joey, I'm so sorry.

He closed the connection for now. All he wanted to do was to lie down beside Autumn and hold her. But he also knew that touching her, just as his dad had said, would mess up the crime scene.

"I'm so sorry this has happened to you, love. If I had any indication that she was out of the hospital, I would never have left you today." He could hear the sirens as he sat there. "They're going to take me away from you. But my mom, she's going to be with you until I can get there. I'll ask my grandda Oliver to be there as well. He loves you as much as I do."

As soon as the police came into his home, knocking open the front door with a battering ram, he told them where he was. When they asked him to stand up, to move away from the body, Joey made sure they understood Autumn wasn't a body but his mate.

"May, Joey. We want you to step away from May. We're going to do this, so nothing comes back to bite you, son. I've already heard from your dad and mom. They told me to tell you they're here for you. I'm going to cuff you now."

As soon as they put the cuffs on him, his dad walked into the door. Unable to hold him, Joey leaned his head onto his father's shoulder and cried. He was sure he wasn't making a great deal of sense, but he was there, and that mattered more to him than most anything would right now. When he lifted his head, Dad wiped his nose. So many fond memories flooded his mind that he was overwhelmed by it.

"You never did have any tissues when you needed one." Dad laughed when he did. "Joey, we've called the hospital, and Evan is going to assist in the surgery. My parents are going too, so they can keep your mom company. Just hang on, son. We'll help you get through this."

Joey was read his rights and then asked if he understood them. When he nodded, someone got him a chair so he could sit down and not be in the way of the medics. He'd not moved Autumn, not even to see if she had a pulse. As soon as she was rolled to her back, he felt his rage surge up around his throat, and he wanted to kill May again.

"They've got this." He nodded at his dad as he put his hand on his shoulder. "I've contacted Nate, the alpha of the wolf pack. He is going to tell Mary Margaret's family and have them go to the hospital with him. Such a shame. She was a wonderful woman."

"She loved Autumn too. When she would come into the kitchen first thing in the morning, she'd have a pot of tea waiting for her. There would be scones or something breakfast like coming out of the oven." They were working hard on Autumn. The medic in charge said they were to take her right to surgery. "Dad, what am I going to do now? I don't want to lose her."

"You're going to be fine, Joey. Both of you are. Just hang on a little while longer, and they'll take her to the hospital. You're doing well. Try and remain calm for a little while longer."

Joey knew of all the people he trusted, which was very few when he thought about it, his dad would keep him calm. He'd talk to him in that calm voice, and Joey's anger would dissipate. Mom would be the one that would get up in peoples' faces if they weren't doing things the way she wanted or even fast enough for her. He knew Mom would make sure Autumn got the best of care. And that no one would ever wonder if Mom would follow through on any threats she'd made. She was like a bear with her cubs.

"Someone needs to contact June and September." Dad said Adrian was going to go there and get them so they'd not have to drive. "Good idea. I don't want anyone else hurt today. Did I tell you Mary Margaret loved Autumn?"

"You did. Now, son, they're going to lift Autumn up and put her on the gurney. Denny wanted me to warn you that it might well hurt her, and she could cry out. They're being as careful as they can, but she'd been beaten up badly." Dad nodded at Denny when Joey said he understood. But as soon as she was lifted, her scream tore through his heart so quickly that without his dad there to hold him back, he was sure he would have hurt his longtime friend. "You're all right. They have her now."

By the time they got her into a waiting ambulance, he was a mess. Joey knew he was repeating himself. He'd caught himself asking Dad where Mary Margaret was three times. When they took him to the cruiser, he bawled like a baby for his dad to not leave him. The officer, Mark, let his dad ride in the front seat with him. Just having him near was a balm to his battered heart.

Mark told him several times before they left his home not to say anything to the press. When asked why they were there, Joey understood. The former president's nephew had killed a woman in fighting for his wife.

There were also a few news crews there just out for something sensational. Anything, he knew, to sell papers or have people watch the news. As soon as they pulled up behind the station house, he was inundated with too many questions for him to answer, even if he had been inclined to do so.

Taken into the station, he was put in a cell at the very back of the house. There was no one around him but his dad. Joey was all right with that. As soon as the door closed to his cell, however, it felt like he was in a deep well with no way out. It took his mom reaching out to him to finally calmed his frayed nerves.

The police have not left the hospital as yet. I wanted you to know the other sisters aren't going to be allowed in here. He told her that was good. *She's going to be in surgery for a while, Joey, so don't worry too much if I don't have news for you. June and September are here, as well and their husbands. Their children are being watched over by the pack.*

Grandda Oliver spoke to him next. *They took a bunch of pictures of her when they got here. Oh, son, I just don't know how someone could do that to such a wonderful person. I will tell you a bit. She has eleven broken ribs, as well as both arms, and her legs are —* Joey told him he didn't want anymore. *I should have thought of that bothering you. She's going to pull through, Joey. Don't you think otherwise. She's going to be home, and it will be just like it never happened.*

His family came to see him off and on. Everyone told him Autumn would pull through, and they'd be all right. Joey didn't know what was going to happen about him killing May. Dad left him for a few minutes to make a call, and it was then that Bennett came to see him.

"You doing all right?" He nodded, then shook his head. "Yeah, I can understand that too. Grandda Oliver told me to give you a hug, but the cops out front said not to get that close to you. They don't think you're going to hurt me, but they do want to make sure that no one thinks I've slipped you something. Stupid if you ask me, but then I'm not in charge."

"You should have seen her, Bennett. She must have been beating her with that bat for a long time. At least it seemed like that to me." Bennett said he'd been by the house, and it was blocked off too. "I figured as much. It's a double homicide, only I did one killing and May the other. Do you know if they found the other sisters? I don't want them anywhere near her. Ever again."

"Mom told me she contacted the oldest one. January, I think her name is. She's livid, Mom said. But you know Mom. She didn't give a shit and told them all to keep away, or she'd make them wish they had. Mom is just as scary now as she was when we were children, and that teacher started treating us badly." Joey nodded, thinking of his mom's anger at her little boys being singled out. "I don't know what's up with Benji, but he's been hiding from all of us since he was picked up from school."

"He's a great kid." Bennett told him how he

was going to work with him on playing baseball. "He mentioned that to me as well. I told him to ask you, as you were the one that had all the athletic ability of the two of us."

"Thank you. I'm looking forward to it." Bennett leaned back but only spoke about things with the kids. Finally, he asked Joey if he was hungry yet. "I can go and get you anything you want. Neal, the guy at the front desk here, said you might be spending the night. I hope to Christ not. That would be hell on all of us knowing you're here without Autumn."

"I'm not really hungry. I was told the same thing. Also that they're following every rule on this, so I don't have to go to prison. I'd surely hate that. It won't hold me, and I won't stay here for killing her." Bennett said he was sure he'd have done the same thing. "Bennett, the bat she had was covered in blood and hair. It was all I could do to just kill her quickly. I wanted her to suffer in the worst kind of way."

Aunt Dylan joined them a little while later. Bennett left to get something to eat when she told him she needed to ask Joey a few questions. Joey told her he honestly didn't remember everything, but he'd be sure to tell her the truth. Aunt Dylan told him he'd better or she'd kick his ass.

"Joey, how did you know to go home?" The little note card was handed to him, and he read it before he looked at her again. "Your dad told us you were at a meeting with him and the others when you said you forgot something at home."

"Yes." He looked at the card again. "I was supposed to pick up some things from the store on my way home. I knew Autumn was going to be out, but her list was long, so I ran home to get it when we had a break." He asked her through their link why he was doing this.

Because you can't say you felt her pain like your own and disappeared from the meeting to end up at your home in time to kill May. This will make it not just sound believable but will keep people thinking how you did it out of their minds. Clearing her throat, she asked her next question. "What do you remember seeing first thing when you entered the home?"

Joey told her about finding Mary Margaret on the floor. "I checked her pulse, and that was how I got her blood on my hand. I didn't know she'd had her throat cut open until that moment." He got a thumbs up from his aunt. "The knife. It was on the floor beside her, I just remembered. I didn't touch it. There were footprints too. I avoided those as well when I entered the dining room from the kitchen."

Joey remembered more detail as he spoke about what he'd done. He didn't remember seeing a car out front when he was there, but he did see one in the back of the house. "Like someone had driven through the yard and right up to the door. I didn't think about that as being odd at the time. I was wholly focused on— I was just picking up my list."

Dad came back when they were winding up the question session. When Aunt Dylan asked him if he remembered anything else, he told her what he thought he'd never forget.

"There was blood everywhere. The ceiling as well as the walls were covered in it. May was laughing. It was manic like she was having a great deal of fun. When I grabbed her from behind, my only thought was to end her hurting my wife." She told him to go on. "I knew Autumn was still alive. I could see her breathing. I was terrified to touch her. I don't know why, but even the thought of checking her pulse scared me. What if I'd not been able to find it? How would I cope without her at my side?"

"You did well, Joey. You did very well with the questions too. I'm working on getting you out of here soon so you can be there with her. Evan said the surgeon is doing a good job of patching her up. It's going to be a while longer, however." He could only nod then, thinking about how much pain she would have been in. "You just sit tight, and I'll see what I can do."

"Hold on a second, Dylan. I've spoken to Henry Cobb. He still has a few strings he can pull being the former president and has fixed it, so Joey is in my custody. When we're together with you, then he's in your care." His aunt thanked his dad. "You're welcome. I thought I'd get him to see Autumn or at least closer, and he'd feel a little better. I know I would."

"Yes. Please. I need to be there when she's awake. Or even just out of surgery."

It took another hour for him to be released into his dad's custody. Driving to the hospital, where Autumn had been life flighted to, seemed to take days instead of the quarter of an hour it actually took. It might well have been longer if not for the police escort the hometown officers had given him to be there sooner rather than later.

"Thank you so much, everyone."

Joey was close to crying again. He didn't think he'd shed this many tears in his entire life. Everyone he'd avoided over the years, the people he'd tried to stay away from, had come to his aid when he needed it most. Family, he'd come to realize in the last few hours, was there for you no matter what sort of ass you were before.

Joey hugged his Grandda Oliver as soon as he was out of the car. "I love you. I thank you for the house and all the treasures we're finding in it. I love you for being the best grandda a man could have. For being there for me. For loving me. But most of all for taking me into your heart and never pushing me out." Grandda hugged him too, the two of them, two big men, hugging each other like they'd never see each other again. "I love you, Grandda, and as much as I know you hate the name, my first son is going to be named for you. Oliver Graham Whitfield."

Before Grandda could tell him no, he left him there in favor of entering the hospital. The elevator was there waiting for him, and there wasn't anyone in it with him. As soon as he got off on the correct floor, he was engulfed in more hugs and more information on Autumn. Joey sat in the waiting room with his family and thanked them for being what they were. The best family in the entire world.

"Evan has been coming in and out since we heard you were coming. He said he'd be out to talk to you soon. He also wanted me to tell you she's going to be fine. She will, however, need to be in the hospital for a few days just to make it look good." He kissed his mom on the cheek and thanked her. "You're so very welcome. I've also made arrangements with the hospital for you to stay here. They're going to put her into a larger bed so that when she's a little longer out of surgery, you can lie beside her. Of course, you'll have to be careful, but I know you will."

"I can't thank you enough for this." She hugged him. "Mom, I've been such a fool for running away. I've come to realize that had I just spoken to you about what I am and what happened to me, I wouldn't have needed to disappear so often."

"You're right. But there is nothing we can do about it now, so we'll just remember that in the future. Correct?" He nodded and smiled at her hard tone. "See that you do. If I have to, Joey Whitfield, I will hunt you down and make you understand how much we love you. Don't leave us again. All right?"

"Yes. All right, Mom. I love you." Nodding, she went to sit down on one of the chairs, and Benji came up to him. "What's up, buddy? I heard you've been hiding from everyone. Tell me what it is, and I'll fix it for you."

"I hurt Aunt Autumn." Joey got down on his knees in front of the boy and hugged him. He didn't know what was going on, but he knew there was no way this child had hurt his aunt. "Will she forgive me, Joey? I didn't mean to give Aunt May the bat."

Chapter 8

Autumn hurt everywhere. She knew this was the second or third time she'd been awake, but this time she knew she wasn't alone in the bed. Reaching behind her to see if it was Joey, her fingers tangled up in curls. Short little ones that could only belong to one person. Opening her eyes, she looked at Joey. He was sitting across from her in the ugliest chair she'd ever seen, smiling at her.

It's Benji. She nodded but was careful of even that movement. *I have to tell you a few things before he wakes up. All right? He feels very responsible for you being hurt. I know what you're going to say — I've said the same thing to him a million times — but he's still feeling that he's failed you. That's the reason he's beside you, and I'm not.*

What is it he thinks he did? Leaning forward, Joey kissed her. She didn't know if he was missing her mouth on purpose for a reason, but the kiss on her forehead was very nice. *Don't distract me. There is a child in my hospital bed, and I want you to tell me. What did he tell you?*

You've been in the hospital for over a week: ten long and boring days. I can tell you now that they were boring because you're awake now. If you are going to stay that way is anyone's guess, but you're awake longer than you've been in a long time. She said his name. *This is important to what I'm going to tell you. Benji has not once left your side. He'll sit on a chair for a little while, but he's been right there since they told us you could have visitors. Benji feels you're going to hate him for the rest of his life because he was supposed to have cleaned up their yard of all the toys before he went to bed the night before. He didn't, leaving not just a bat outside where anyone could pick it up but also all the toys he'd just gotten. From you, I have to add.*

I'm assuming that was what was used to hurt me. Was it May? He nodded and told her she got both of them right. *He thinks it's his fault for leaving the bat out so May could pick it up and use it? He does know I will love him forever, doesn't he?*

No. He does think, and no one can convince him otherwise, that once he tells you what he's done and how it was his fault, you're going to order him from your life again, and he'll never get to see you. His reasoning is because you never saw him before, and now he's messed up — his words, not mine — you're going to hate him forever for almost getting you killed. Autumn didn't know what to say. Well, she did, but she doubted Benji would appreciate her knocking him around a bit to see reason. *His mom took him home yesterday to get a bath and change his clothing. He packed his stuff up, but nothing you and I bought him in the way of toys. I don't know his plan, but he also cleaned up all the toys in the yard, and his room is neat as a pin, she told me. It's breaking her heart too that he won't believe her when she tells him he's going to be just fine.*

Where is your dad in all this? Joey asked her why. *He needs to talk to this boy. Benji has a dad in his life, but none of these kids have had a grandda. Blake needs to come and get this boy, take him out for ice cream or whatever he does with his grandkids, and tell him like a man that he's going to be just fine.*

Why can't you help? She told him she would, but that Benji needed to hear it from someone older, someone who had been around the block a few times. *I bet my dad will have a story pretty much just like the one Benji has about what happened. Maybe not to the point where you were, but close.*

I'm sure that he does. This is what I'm wanting you to do for him. I'm going to pretend to still be out. You have your dad come and get him and have a talk. Tell him not to lie to him, like make up a story to fit, but to tell him about something harsh. She thought about the story of Blake and Ronald, another kid Blake hadn't adopted. However, she didn't know if Joey knew. Autumn kept it to herself. *Then, while he's out, you'll let him know I'm awake, and they can come back after he talks to him. I promise you, this is just what Benji, as well as your dad, needs. A man to man talk about making mistakes and what happens when you own up to the truth.*

While he's out, you'll tell me what you know about Ronald. She told him she wouldn't do that. It was up to his dad to tell him. *Is it my dad's fault?*

No. Of course not. But he thinks it is like Benji feels my being hurt was his. Joey stared at her for several seconds, and she let him. *I promise you, this is just what they both need.*

She laid there as Benji woke, and he and Joey spoke quietly. She found out a few things by listening to them. The funeral for May was over, and she'd been buried in the same cemetery her parents were going to be. That no one other than January, February, and July had been there. There hadn't been any flowers sent. No one from the Whitfield family had gone either. But, by contrast, Mary Margaret's funeral had been huge.

"I ain't never seen so many people than there were out there in those woods, Uncle Joey. Did you see all that food too?" Joey told Benji they were a close community, and they came together when needed. "Grandpa Blake told me the food was all cooked by the ladies of the pack and that when they were all done eating, they'd take the leftovers to the nursing home you guys own. That's really nice. I don't think other nursing homes eat that good, do you?"

Joey laughed. "No. It's doubtful even restaurants feed people that well. But it was good food. Did you eat much?" Benji said he'd not been too hungry lately. "Benji, she'll love you no matter what. You have to know that."

"I hope so, but she was hurt really bad, Uncle Joey. She could have died on account of me not picking up my toys when Momma told me to. I will forever, from now on. No matter where I go." Joey asked him where he was going when Blake came into the room. "Hi, Grandpa Blake. We was talking about the food at Mary Margaret's funeral."

A change in subject. An avoidance of having two people telling Benji he was going to be all right. Autumn wanted to wake up then, tell him she loved him but knew this was what Blake needed as well.

The two of them left, though Benji was very reluctant to do so, on the premise of getting lunch and bringing it back. She opened her eyes as soon as the door closed behind them and looked at Joey. He was a man she would love forever, and she didn't think she could do any better if she'd planned him out all on her own.

"I have something I need to tell you too. Something you won't have known from when you were hurt. I'm the one that killed May. She had killed Mary Margaret before finding you when she did. The bat she used on you had been used to break in the back door. It wasn't until they took Mary Margaret's body away that they realized why she'd not heard the break in. She'd had been listening to music when the glass was broken. Had she been in the hospital with a team of doctors around her, the medical examiner said she still would have died.

I'm sorry." She asked him if he was sorry for killing May. "No. I've thought about that too—a great deal. But no, I'm not sorry she's dead or that I killed her. I'm only sorry I broke her neck instead of making her suffer."

"What else is there? You have more to tell me." He nodded. "All right. Tell me, or so help me, when I'm able, I'm going to strip you naked, and then I'm going to be naked and tease you until you burst."

Joey laughed. It was just what she needed, and obviously, he did as well. When he took her hand into his, he kissed the back of it and looked into her eyes. She could see his sadness there, and it hurt her beyond anything she'd ever felt before.

"You were pregnant." She hurt. Just those three little words made everything in her world come crashing down on her heart. When she heard Joey say her name, she could only stare at him through tears. To have had and lost hurt her. "Had it been born and taken its first breath, the beating wouldn't have hurt the child. We can try again, he told me. It was a combination of the stress of you're being hurt as well as the medications they used to save your life. And even had I been able to give you enough blood, there wouldn't have been any saving our child. The little baby was, like your womb, damaged horrifically in the beating. But with my help and that of the hospital, you're going to be just fine. We're going to be just fine."

They both cried for what seemed like a long time.

Someone came in and left them to grieve. Holding onto Joey, her lifeline, she told him how very sorry she was that she'd not been able to save their baby. He told her that had she died or even not been able to live a full life, it would have left him with nothing in his heart anyway. But that as soon as she was home again, they'd have dozens of children if she wanted.

"I do. Yes. I don't know about dozens, but I do want children with you." He nodded and held her, climbing into the bed behind her, Joey wrapped her not just in her arms but his love too.

The two of them talked about the things they were going to do when they left here. How they were going to work on projects that would keep them happy. The things they were taking over for his parents would be enough to keep them busy for decades. Then they spoke about all the things she'd missed while, as he put it, she napped away their time.

The staff came in and out of the room with them. No family was notified that she was awake yet. It was their time to heal. They'd both taken a blow to their hearts, and she knew it was going to take them time to get their hearts to not hurt so much. She knew it would hurt her forever to know she'd lost her first child with the man she loved.

~~~

Blake loved the kids that were around so much now. He didn't know June or September's children well, but he loved them. Shadow had taken to calling them her grandbabies too, and he was all right with that. Blake would love them all if he was able. But he also knew this little guy was stressed out.

He could also taste it on his skin, the struggle he was going through. While he wasn't sure what it was, he was positive it had something to do with his Aunt Autumn. When Joey asked him if he'd help him, Blake knew that today would be the turning point for both of them.

As they waited on their pizza to be brought to them, Blake reached out and touched the mind of the child. It was right there, right in his head, that he'd been the one responsible for Autumn being hurt. Blake thought for sure he was in over his head when he remembered one other child he'd not helped.

"Benji, I have something I need to tell you. Something I've never told anyone else but my own dad. Not even Shadow knows." Benji looked up at him, his face so sad that Blake wanted to pull him into his arms and hold him. Hold him until everything in the world was right again. "When I adopted your uncles, Joey and Bennett, there was another little boy that was to come to me. His name was Ronald Gipson. He was a little older than Bennett. I believe he was fourteen at that time. But I didn't take him."

"Was he a bad person?" Blake started to tell him he had been but told him he was misunderstood instead.

"I don't know what that means. Did they not know how to talk to him?"

"Yes. That's basically it. He didn't have anyone to listen to him. And those that did try, they didn't hear what he was saying to them." Benji looked more confused. "He tried to tell the people who were trying to care for him that he had something — he said someone — in his head telling him to be a terrible person. He called himself terrible, so in turn, the people believed him. Some of the things he'd done, they were terrible. Ronald killed two people while trying to get away from the police. He also stole things — food for the most part — and that was something that got him into trouble. The boy was starving."

"My mom told my brothers and I that we weren't to tell people we were starving most of the time before Aunt Autumn came to help us." He played with his napkin. "I didn't mean for her to be hurt, Grandpa. I never should have not did what my momma wanted me to do and pick up my toys."

Blake moved over to the other side of the table and picked him up. Putting him on his lap, Blake was able to make it so the rest of the restaurant didn't see them. Didn't hear the heartfelt confessions Benji was making. Holding him, Blake felt his own eyes fill with tears as he felt his own heart hurt for his own folly at being a failure for someone.

When he was calmed down a little more, Blake held him. "Ronald was killed two weeks after I didn't take him. He had wanted help, you see, and thought he might get it from me. I didn't help him. Just like you didn't help your momma by picking up your toys. I didn't kill Ronald. You didn't hurt your aunt either. But, like you, I've always felt as if it was my fault. It took me years of hurt to get over that. Years of not being able to talk about him without feeling like a failure. It wasn't until my dad took me aside and made me tell him what happened that I realized the truth."

Joey didn't eat any of the pizza when it was brought to them. Sitting him in the chair beside him, Blake tried to get his mind straight so he could tell the little boy what had gone down. What had happened to end the life of someone so young. Putting a slice of the pizza on both their plates, he thought about his words and decided to be as straightforward as his own father had been to him.

"My dad told me that had I taken the boy in, he might well have not been starving all the time. He would have had a roof over his head and family around him. But, and he told me this was the most important thing of all, he would have been just a timebomb ready to explode at any moment. He might well have killed more people because he was around all of us all the time." Benji looked at him like he had all the answers in the world. "Ronald had a tumor in his brain that made him angry all the time. He would work to not show it as hard as he could, but there was no hiding it all the time. In order to make himself be this person he wasn't, Ronald took to killing small animals, then larger ones, to satisfy his need to soften his anger. But as the anger grew, so did his need to kill."

Benji picked up the pizza and took a bite. Blake was so happy he took one himself. He thought of the people that had been murdered simply because they'd been in the wrong place at the wrong time. As he continued his story, he felt his own heart lighten of the burden of guilt.

"Just after he was put in a home, not a family home but a home with people, they started to discipline him. To make him do chores around the house. Nothing terrible, but just things like taking out the trash. Putting his clothing away. Ronald's rage, because by then it was rage, got out of control. He murdered the two of them because he couldn't live with himself any longer." Benji asked him if he'd been with nice people. "As it turned out, he was. They were nice to him. Gave him what they thought he needed. But it was too late for him by then. The tumor in his head was growing and pressing against everything in his brain that was making him hurt. The pain, you see, felt like someone was talking to him, and he didn't know the difference."

"I feel sorry for him." Blake said he did as well. "Do you think you would have found the tumor sooner?"

"No. I might well have, but probably not. You see, I wouldn't have known he was ill because he would have smelled the same to me as he always did. Had I smelled him before the tumor got in his head, I would have known the difference in him. But as it was, I didn't take the chance on him. Fearful, you see, of him hurting someone in my family." Benji stared at him. Blake could see his mind working. "I have always felt like it was my fault because I didn't take him into my heart."

"This is like my Aunt May. I didn't know she was going to take my bat. I didn't even know she was out of the hospital." Benji played with his napkin again. "Momma told us she was sick and would die soon. She wasn't in my head when I didn't want to pick up my stuff. I just didn't want to do it. Like you didn't want to take the chance on Ronald." Benji looked up at him. "You did the right thing, Grandpa. I know you would have helped him if you could have, but like my momma is telling us all the time, God has a plan, and if it's for you not to do something or get something, then that's the way it should be. I never thought of that until right now. Aunt May took my bat and hurt Aunt Autumn, but she could have hurt her with anything. Right?"

"Yes. She could have had a gun and hurt her worse than she did with the bat." Benji nodded. "Do you understand what I'm trying to tell you, Benji? That not listening to your momma isn't a good thing, but it's not the reason your aunt was hurt. Nor the reason May was killed. It happened this way to someone like your aunt that cannot die. May didn't kill anyone else but Mary Margaret, when it could have been so much worse. Killing that nice woman was a terrible thing, don't get me wrong. But your leaving your bat out and her finding it isn't— Benji, I just thought of something else. She was at your home. What if May had gone into your house to look for something to hurt Autumn with? She might well have killed you all before she went to see Autumn. You leaving your bat outside for her to find, it more than likely saved all your lives."

"Just like Ronald not being at your house did for your family." Right there was what he'd needed. Right there was the thing Blake had needed to hear all his life in dealing with this. "You left your own bat outside—you know, by not taking him to your house—and you saved your own family and the pack from Ronald hurting them too. Grandpa, you're wonderful."

Blake felt that way too. Just as he was reaching for another slice of pizza, Blake heard from his son. Autumn was awake and talking. Not only that, but she didn't seem to have any kind of brain damage from the beating. After telling Benji that, the two of them hugged for a full ten minutes before he was ready to talk again.

Also, Blake had a better understanding, a clear understanding, of the relationship between Joey and his own grandfather. He knew then why it was an old man Joey had gone to when he needed it. Age did make a difference in this sort of relationship.

~~~

Joey could see the difference in both his dad and Benji. He was still tender, the little boy, but he was much happier at finding out his aunt didn't blame him for what had happened. Dad asked to speak to him, and he met him in the hallway across from Autumn's room. While standing there, not only did he tell him the story of Ronald, but he thanked him for asking him to take care of little Benji. Joey didn't know what to say.

"I know now that I couldn't have helped him. I also need for you to know I would have tried had I been a single man without you and your brother there." Joey told him he was glad he had them there then. "I am as well. While I'm an immortal, I know that now— No, now I understand that even had I taken him in, he would still have died. I know that even with my help, he was still going to be in pain."

"Dad, I can't tell you enough about how much I love you." They hugged—it was beginning to be a habit with them, this hugging. It was something Joey vowed to do with everyone from now on. "I love you, old man. With all my heart."

"And I love you too." He looked at the door that had his family behind it. His wife there as well. "Did you tell her about the baby?"

"Yes." When he didn't ask more about it, Joey didn't give him more information. It was enough, he thought, that his dad had asked. And that he'd taken care of it. When they hugged again before going into the room, Grandda Oliver came out to see if they were all right. "Yes, we're wonderful. How about you?"

"He just called me an old man, Dad. What the hell am I supposed to do with someone who does that?" Grandda huffed. "You think he should be able to call me that?"

"You are an old man, son. I'm sorry to break it to you, but you're very old." They all laughed, the three of them. "I was wondering if you talked to Autumn. I know it's a tender subject, but I didn't want her to be upset anymore and was wondering."

"I told her. We're going to try again." Grandda asked him if he was still going to name his son for him. "Yes. I'm going to do it. I've not spoken to Autumn about that, but once she figures out that you won't like it, she'll be all for it."

"Figures." Grandda looked at his dad. "He calls you an old man and disrespects me like this. I tell you, Blake, there is no point in having children anymore. They just treat you like crap all the time."

"So you don't want me to have children of my own?" Grandda looked so shocked by the notion that Joey laughed. "We are, Grandda. I want to see Autumn fat with my child."

"I'd not call her fat if I was you. I did that to your granny once, and she durn near took my head off. Delicate. You need to remember that word. It's going to come up, her asking you if you think she's fat. Don't say it. Just tell her how delicate she looks." Grandda laughed. "You'll have me some great grandbabies, Joey. They'll be just like your lady wife in there. I hope so, I surely do."

That thought scared him just a little. To have children running around as magical as the two of them would be so frightening. But he did laugh a little. At least they were all immortal, and that would help a great deal.

Dylan had called him yesterday. The police had everything they needed and had cleared him of all charges. Joey had never been so happy about news before. Even the officer in charge of the crime had called later to thank him for his cooperation and to ask after Autumn. He wouldn't, they told him, have to worry about a trail either as it was all cleared up.

Mom ordered food for them, and the entire family showed up. Well, not all of them, but his uncles and their wives. It was a good time to have them all around. Food and family were about the best things a man could have. Joey decided he was going to make a difference in some children's lives as his own dad had done for him. Excusing himself for a few moments, Joey found himself in the nursery of the hospital.

"Mr. Whitfield? I was just going to call your father. Did you hear about the babies?" Shaking his head, he told her he'd been celebrating with his family and had decided he needed a moment. "There isn't any place on earth more wonderful than sitting in a room full of babies. Come on in. Tell me what you think of these two little ones we got in here. Brother and a sister. They've been turned over to the state, and we were just trying to find them a home to take them for a few days."

He only needed to know they needed him, and he was sold on taking them home. Twice he wanted to talk to Autumn about it, and both times one of them would do something that would pull at his heart. They weren't even named yet. Their mother had said she wasn't in a position to take care of twins and had signed them over. Joey sat down with them in his arms when he finally got around to talking to Autumn. All he did was say he needed to ask her something.

I'll take them. He laughed, startling the babies awake, so they stared at him. *Bring them up now, Joey. There isn't any reason whatsoever that they shouldn't be a part of this family.*

The nurse told him she'd help, and he found himself being loaded up with all the things he'd need for a night at home with them. As he was being told what else he'd need, they were on the elevator and on their way up to the room. Before going in, he asked the nurse, Mary, to hang on a second. He needed to push them in on his own. Mary said she understood him completely.

Pushing the bassinette into the room, he was met with silence. He knew it wouldn't last, so he picked up his daughter and laid her in the arms of Autumn. Picking up his son, he laid him down beside her in the oversized bed without commenting to anyone. It was his dad who spoke first.

"What do you have there, son?" He pulled the

blanket off the little boy and asked if he knew what it was. "Looks like a baby you got there. You planning something?"

"I'm planning to take them home with me. What do you think?" Dad picked up the boy and handed him to Mom. Dad asked if he could have the little girl, and Autumn handed her off to him. There was still no one talking in the room yet. "I know the little boy's name. He's Oliver Graham Whitfield. But I'm still trying to decide on a little girl's name for my daughter."

It was Benji that spoke up. "Mary Margaret Luna Whitfield. I'm gonna call her Me-Me." Autumn told him that was perfect. "Good. I'm going to teach her all kinds of stuff. But she's going to be picking up her toys when she's told. What is she, Uncle Joey?"

It took him a second to realize what Benji was asking. Grandda told him she was a tiger, but an orange one. Everyone then seemed to wake up. Another tiger in the family. Another child for them to care for. Joey couldn't have been happier if he had a dozen children, all of them as different as he was happy.

Chapter 9

Autumn looked around the prison while she waited for her parents to be brought out. She was going to talk to them and not let them bother her. Since she'd brought the babies home and had healed, not just her body, but her heart and mind too, she knew she was going to have to talk to them once more. It was the things Dylan had told her that she was going to talk to them about.

Her dad was brought out first. Then a few minutes later, her mother was. Neither of them looked as if they were happy to see her.

"I don't care what your complaints are. Nor do I give a shit how much you think you've been wronged. I'm here to let you know a few things that have been kept from you. Also, a few things that are going to be done for you from now on. Are you willing to listen or not? Frankly, I could care less, but it's up to you." They looked at each other, then nodded at her. "All right. I don't know if you were told or not, but May is dead. She was killed when she tried to murder someone else."

"We know it was you. Why you didn't just die instead of her, we'll never know." Just what she expected them to say to her. It didn't even bother her anymore. They were, as far as she was concerned, no longer relevant to her. "What else? We have things to do too, in the event you didn't know that."

"I'm aware of what you're here doing. January killed herself the night before last. She left a note saying she could no longer live without her best friend. I'm assuming, as did the police, that she meant May. She shot herself with one of her husband's many guns he had around the house." Both of them cried for that. The guards that had come out with them handed them a box of tissues. The next part was going to be more difficult for them. "February is in a mental institution. She'll remain there for the rest of her life. Like January, she left a note when she tried to kill herself too and said basically the same thing. That she could no longer live without May. She'd cut her wrists, but her husband, who was cleaning out his things from the house as he was leaving her, found her before it was too late. There was some brain damage done, and she will need specialized care for the remainder of her life. I'm making sure she gets the best of care."

"She's our little girl. You'd better make sure she gets care. How could you?" Autumn didn't bother answering her mother. Since she'd had nothing to do with any of this, she was only going to let them blame her. They would have anyway. There was still one more child she was going to have to make them understand about if there was going to ever be any understanding of someone trying to take their own life. "I suppose July is the only child we have left now. Except for you. Not that we consider you a child of ours."

"I don't care. I honestly could care less what you think of me as your child. July, I'm sorry to say, is gone as well. She killed her husband and tried to murder her children. Her children are going to come and live with Joey and I as soon as they're released from the hospital. July shot her husband and then took the children out to the car with her and left the engine running in the garage. She killed herself with the same gun she'd killed her husband with. The children would have died as well if not for a nosey neighbor coming to check on them."

Her parents were devastated by then. Joey had asked to come with her, and she wished now that she'd had him come. But he was home with their children and was going to meet her at the door with them. It was the best way, she knew, to end this nightmare of a day. She continued speaking as they reeled from what she was telling them.

"February had a will made out, and her children will go to their father. January's children are older and are going to be staying with us as well. They've been living with their father for some time now. I had no idea they were divorced. As he is ill, dying of Hodgkin's, he has signed custody over to Joey and I. He will be visiting them from time to time, but—"

"You're to get us out of here so we can raise our grandchildren. There is no way they'd be happy knowing you have them." Autumn told her father no. "What do you mean, no? I'm your father, and you will do what I tell you."

"This might have escaped your memory, but I don't care a thing for you either. I don't think I ever did. So you trying to get me to do anything you say is just not going to happen. I'm going to raise these children because I have the means and the heart to do so. If you don't like it? Well, you can fuck off for all I care. So you understand too. I'm not going to tell them whatever fabricated stories their mothers did about the two of you. They'll know why you're here and why I won't come to see you. Fucking shut up so I can get this over with, or you'll be left in the dark about a lot of things." Mother said she hated her. "Well, that's wonderful. We finally agree on something. The insurance February had is going to cover her expenses. Joey and I are going to make sure she is, as I said, getting the best of care. The other two have been buried next to May in the same cemetery you two are going to."

"You're a cold bitch." Autumn thanked her father. "That wasn't to make you happy, you dumb ass, but to insult you."

"I don't care. Perhaps you should remember that when you toss around insults you think might hurt me. I have twins now. A boy and a little girl. They're going to know things you never gave me. Love, understanding, and the meaning of family. Not that you're going to care, but I'm just putting that out there. There is now money in your accounts here. There will be from now on. Every Monday, there will be a box sent to you with things in it that you might well need. Nothing expensive—as I said, I don't like you—but things you will need for your lives in prison. I don't care if you use it or trade it. It's there for you. And before you think this is my idea, it's not. June and September, other children you have and didn't ask about, asked me to do this. The box will contain useful items, but no pictures of the grandchildren or the rest of us. There will be no cards at Christmas or your birthdays, nor will you be able to call any of us in hopes of getting news. This today is all you're ever going to get. The rest is none of your business. Do you have any questions?"

"Why are you here and not one of the other two?" She told them what June and September had told her, that they wanted nothing to do with them. "What a horrible bunch of children we had. If not for the other five, I would have thought we'd be better off smothering the lot of you."

Autumn had told them what she'd come to say to them. But instead of feeling relieved, she was more hurt than before. She'd known it would hurt, but the reality of it was more than just a little painful. Standing up, she looked down at them both.

"One more thing I want to tell you, then you'll never see any one of us again. You could have had so much right now. You could have been in the lives of your children and their husbands. The eleven grandchildren that are ours could have been giving you comfort in your later years, but you've flushed it away. Family means so much more to me than it did before. Having someone there, all the time, that you can lean on has been the best treasure of all. You fucked it over by being what you are. Mean, selfish people that only give a damn about what you want and what things are given to you." Autumn shook her head. "When you die, this place has been told what to do with your bodies. There will be no coming together of us to see you off. You fucked that up when you shoved us all away. No marker will tell people where you are, what sort of people you were. Nothing in a way of reminding others you were a part of this world. When you die, it will be as if you never existed. Never had a part in our lives. Just two people that tried to murder someone a long time ago and were forgotten."

They were still screaming at her when she walked out the door. Turning in her badge, she stood out in the sunshine and let the slight breeze blow the smell of the prison and the two people there off her skin. The warmth of it was better than she'd ever gotten from the two people that had brought her into this world.

Autumn put herself in the babies' bedroom. The house was filled now, and she loved it. Even with the extra people, there didn't seem to be a great deal of noise that she had to take care didn't bother the babies. Picking up Ollie, she held him in her arms until she felt calm enough to talk to him and his sister.

"They're not at all nice people. Just so you know. And the very fact I had to go there again ticked me off something terrible." She looked up to see Robin standing in the doorway. She was the oldest child here at seventeen and was January's child. "Would you like to hold him? Or even Me-Me?"

"No thanks. Why did you take us in?" She asked her what she meant. "I'm going to be eighteen soon, and I could have stayed with Curt in a home for those few months. You didn't have to take us in. I would have thought you had enough children here, what with the new babies and all."

"I know that, but I needed you to be here with me. To know you're all right. Are you?" She shrugged. "See? You're not all right. Come here, hold a baby. It's very calming."

"Mom hated you. I'm not at all sure why—I don't think she knew either. But when we were growing up, she would spew her anger daily about how you'd done this or that as a child. We looked some of it up, figuring there might be something in the paper about how you'd tried to murder her. Or you had robbed a bank. There was never anything." Autumn didn't know how to answer but let Robin speak. She came into the room and took Me-Me from her bed. Then she sat on the floor with her. "Curt and I avoided her after we got to read what really was in the paper. There was very little about you doing anything but plenty to say about what had been done to you. I'm sorry for that."

"Thank you, Robin, but it wasn't anything you could have known about." She nodded as she laid the baby on the floor and unwrapped the blanket around her. When she played with her toes, Autumn had to smile. "Did you give any thought to the things left at the house for you to take?"

"Yes. The things from my room, for the most part. A few things of my dad's, if you'll be all right with that." She nodded, hurting for the kids left behind in all this. "You went to see the grandparents today. How was that? Or have you answered my question by talking to Ollie?"

"It was done, and that's all I wanted out of it. They're aware of the deaths. So many in such a short amount of time. I wonder if they planned it, to all die like they did." Robin told her they more than likely had. They had a plan for every little thing. "I'm beginning to understand that. Did you get the message from your Aunt June? I think she has a job for you."

"Yes. I'm going to be working with her at the shop she's taken a job at. It looks like it'll be fun. I have to tell you, Aunt Autumn, I love your mother-in-law. She's a pistol, as my dad would have said of her." Robin looked so hurt then that Autumn wasn't surprised when she changed the subject. "I'm also going to do some babysitting for the aunts. You too, if you ever find the time to go out with Uncle Joey. Man, he's a good looking man."

"He is at that. He has an entire family of good looking men. Even the grandparents." The two of them sat and talked about the Whitfield family. Robin wasn't at all like her brother. Curt was a jokester, as well as a very happy person. He hadn't mentioned his parents once since he'd been brought here. Also, she noticed that he and Benji, for some reason, hung out a great deal. More than likely, she thought, it was Benji hanging out with him.

After the babies were changed and put back to bed, she and Robin made their way to the kitchen. It was, she'd noticed, becoming the meeting place. Autumn wasn't the least bit surprised to find not just Benji there but also his little brother Phil. Curt joined them in the kitchen just as she was answering the house phone.

"Don't you have a home?" Benji told Curt he did. "You're always here. Are you gonna move in here too, little guy? I mean, I'm sure we can stuff you someplace." The smile, so his mother's, hurt Autumn while she was listening to the woman on the other end. When she hung up, she looked around the room at the kids.

"Mrs. Maple was on her way here, and her car broke down. Are any of you going to be here for the next forty-five minutes or so? I need someone to watch the children." Robin said she wasn't going anywhere until four when she had to be at work. "All right. Will you keep an eye on things for me?"

"Sure." Autumn handed her the baby monitor. "Where are you going, Curt? Remember, you have to go fill out the paperwork if you want to play football this fall."

Autumn left them to it. It was nice, she thought, having all the hustle and bustle of the household now. Even Joey had said he didn't mind the crowd around the table as much as he thought he would. As she drove to where Mrs. Maple had told her she was, she remembered Joey was going to get both Robin and Curt a car to drive. It would certainly help her getting them all going in the morning once school started up again.

~~~

Joey entered the kitchen just as Curt and Robin were arguing. He, for the most part, stayed out of their fights. He knew that kids fought, and these two had been under a great deal of stress for the last several weeks. When Curt said he was going to take a walk, Robin told Joey where Autumn had gone and that she was caring for the kids.

"Thank you for that. Will you keep track of how much we ask you to do that? I want to make sure you get some spending money for it. Also, I don't know if Autumn mentioned it, but we're going to get you and Curt a car."

Hope. Had he not been looking at her when he said it, it would have been gone too soon. Stirring his cup of tea, he sat down at the big table he'd only just had cleaned. It had had blood on it when—

"Do you know much about the college around here?" He asked her what she wanted to do. "I'm not sure now. My plans had been to be a teacher, but I don't know if the local college will offer much in the way of classes I need. I'm also going to see about double majoring. I would love to teach a secondary language."

"That's a great idea. But if you don't mind me asking, why are you going to go to the local college rather than, say, Ohio State? Either one is a good college, but don't second guess yourself because of it." He remembered the envelope that had been on the table all this time. Joey had finally opened it a couple of days ago. "Hang on a minute."

He came back to the room, and she was on her cell phone. When she handed it over to him, Joey was slightly confused. It was about her bill and who was going to be paying it. Joey told the lady, who he thought was rude, that he'd take care of it today.

"We'll put you guys on our plan. My family, that includes you guys now, has this great rate. You go with me when I go, and you can get a phone. I did notice yours was slightly outdated." She asked him if he was serious. "I am. There is no point in making you use a phone you've obviously had for some time. Besides, I want to know it'll work when you need to get in touch with me. All right. OSU has asked me to come and teach at the university. According to the paperwork I was sent, I'm going to be teaching botany. I have a doctorate in it, and the offer couldn't have come at a better time. In fact, there is a perk I think you might like. At least, I think you will. It says any child of mine can go to college for free. Not including books."

She looked at him and a tear formed in her eye. "I'm not your daughter, Uncle Joey. I mean, it's really a great perk for your children. Me-Me and Oliver will really need that in the future. But I doubt very much you'd want to call us your children when we're going to be here for only a little while." He asked her what she meant. "I don't know about your family, Uncle Joey, but adopted children aren't treated like real children."

"Robin, honey, I'm adopted." She frowned at him. "So is Bennett and a great many other family members that are a part of this family. Even Me-Me and Oliver are. The Whitfield family doesn't just love their own children, they love hard for all the children brought to this family. My grandda, he didn't adopt any of his boys, but he certainly treated those adopted by his sons as if they were born of his blood. He calls them children of his heart. I think that's what you've become to all of them here as well."

"I had no idea." She looked at Benji, who was sitting there listening to them. She smiled at the little boy. "You're not adopted, but I know for a fact you call them all your grandparents. Did you know Joey was adopted?"

"Sure." He rolled his eyes at her. "You know, for a girl, you're pretty dense. Uncle Bennett doesn't even look like Uncle Joey. And the babies upstairs, they're cats, but they're orange, not white. Did you know they're white tigers? I knew that a long time ago."

Joey went over the perks with her that he had coming to him. One of them was a car. He also pointed out to her that she, because he was a professor there, could live off campus the first year. She looked a little disappointed about that, so he made a mental note to find a dorm she could stay in here where he knew she'd be safe. They were still talking about it when Curt joined them. He looked pale, and Joey stood up, feeling his beasts roll over him.

"There is a lady out in the yard. She's got wings — like not fake ones, either. She said you were supposed to meet with her today." Joey said he'd forgotten. "You forgot that you're supposed to meet a woman, a very beautiful one at that, with wings? Uncle Joey, you've been married way too long."

Aurora appeared in the room with them. She was smiling at them all, and he could see the healthy bit of glow that surrounded her. Introducing her to his children, she touched each of them. Joey knew, even if the kids didn't that she'd given them a bit of magic they'd figure out sooner or later.

"I've come to speak to you about something." She looked at Curt, and Joey realized he was dazed a little. "I've since decided I'd like to take this one with me for a bit, please. He will be a nice addition to my staff if you'd not mind. Joey, he has ideas in this head I believe will help me a great deal with the planting."

"You'd have to talk to him about it, Aurora. But he has to finish his education too." She said she'd work around that for him. "Autumn will also need to approve it for you. I don't see a problem with it, so long as he knows you can zap him if he screws up."

"You have magic?" Curt laughed. "I guess you do. I mean, it's not every day a faerie queen just pops in and out of the yard like you did without having a bit of magic."

"I want to help too." Curt surprised Joey by asking Aurora if she had something for Benji to do. "Yeah. I'm his best buddy. Me and Curt, we're a team, huh Curt?"

"Sure we are, buddy. A good team." Aurora looked at Joey, and he was glad to have the opportunity to explain how Curt had done something special. "You mean simply because I was willing to share my job with my little cousin, I've gotten a boon from the queen? I don't really need anything, my lady. I've not been able to spend a great deal of time with any of my cousins, and I'm just enjoying having someone around that makes me feel like I'm not as bad as I've been led to believe."

"Our mom." Robin hugged her brother. "You're the best. I want you to know that. And Uncle Joey, I'd love to be one of your perks and go to college. I never thought, in all my thoughts about having to live here with you guys, that I'd have so much. Not just a family to call my own, but an education I was told I'd never need, as well as someone to believe in me."

Joey felt like he could take on the world and come out not just on top but as a king of it all. Never, in all his own dreams, had he thought he'd be sharing his home with so many children. Not even having so many of his own. But here they were with not just kids to keep them company, but also ones that made him feel like he could do this.

Dad. His dad told him he was waiting on his call to help. Laughter spilled from his mind. *I love you. I love you so very much.*

Thank you, son. That was unexpected but needed. What's going on? Anything I can help you with? I'm asking because I'd love to come to help out with all the kids. Especially the twins. Joey told him he'd love to have him there whenever he wanted. *I'm happy to hear that. Very happy. I have to admit, I was sitting here feeling sorry for myself a little. You are there raising all those wonderful children, and I'm here, sitting in an empty home with no one to talk to.*

Dad, you're sounding a bit whiney. Why don't you come over, we'll gather up all the kids, and you can help me pick out cars for the two drivers I have in my growing family? Robin is going to go to OSU, and Curt is working with Aurora. While I don't know what he's going to be doing with her, I'm sure it will be fun.

When Dad showed up to go with him, Autumn had made it home and was going to stay with the babies. He was glad for that. Joey had nightmares about the car seats. Not to mention, he had no idea how he was going to fit everyone in the car with him.

Dad took Curt and Benji with him, and Joey had Robin in his car. They'd need to get an oversized van, he realized, just to take them all with them if they went to dinner. He added that to his mental list of things to get finished up today.

Joey hadn't understood the meaning of family until he'd met and fallen in love with Autumn. He'd not understood the things he'd been missing out on when he'd gone away. Knowing how badly he'd treated those who had loved him unconditionally made him want to do something special for them. He didn't know what it would be, but he'd do it.

The car Robin picked out even made his dad cringe. It was practical, it was used, and it looked like it was older than he was. When he told her he needed for her to be safe, Joey took them to the new car section.

"I need to know that when you leave the house,

you'll be able to return. And if you're running errands for us, perhaps with one of the others in your car, you'll be able to keep them safe as well. Also, traveling back and forth to college is going to be expensive as it is with gas. We'd rather you had something that was going to get good gas mileage, as well as provide heat and air when you need it." She looked once again at the car he would have picked out for her. "Tell me what it is you want, and we can go from there. If you don't, then I'm going to let my dad pick it out."

"What would you get for me, Grandpa?" Dad looked like he was going to explode with happiness when she called him grandpa. Dad, not speaking, took her to the little yellow car Robin had been looking at. "I love the color too. I want it, but it's too much. I mean, really too much."

"I want nothing but the best for my granddaughter." Robin hugged Joey tightly, then his dad. When she touched the car with her hands, like it was made of blown glass, they knew she'd be driving that sucker all the time.

Curt was just a little harder to nail down. He wanted a red truck. Dad wasn't keen on him having a red one, but he did agree with his idea of how useful it would be to have a truck. As the two of them walked away, Benji started to tag along but stopped just short of it. The little guy looked up at him.

"Can I have a car when I learn to drive, Uncle Joey?" He asked him what sort he'd want. "Just like

Curt's. Maybe he'll teach me to drive, and I'll be safe too. I can take the babies out when I'm older, huh?"

"I've had a talk with Curt here on red. He's decided he'd like to have a neutral color so as not to get into too much trouble when he's driving. I told him about your little red troublemaker and how many times you were pulled over for it when you were at home." He asked Curt what he considered neutral. "We think green will be the best, right, Curt?" Dad was in his element. He had someone hanging on his every word.

"The green one is a little pricy. But I really do like it. It has a few more features on it that the red one didn't. I think if you told them you were going to buy other cars, you might get that one for a little less." Joey asked him how he'd come to that. "I saw Aunt Shadow do it the other day when she was buying steaks for the family. The man was so impressed he threw in two more at no charge for her haggling with him. She told me later that people expect that. I think hanging around with her might be good for me."

Joey didn't want to think about how much his mom could teach this kid. Cursing came to mind. Also, she'd be able to teach him good things, such as finding a good bargain. Loving the way things were working out, he was thrilled that Curt had been right. He got a good deal on all the cars, including the super-sized van he got for when they were all together.

After they were finished shopping for cars, the

bunch of them picked up pizzas and headed for home. Dad called over Mom, and her and Dad fed the babies while the rest of them sat around the table. This was what it was supposed to be like, he realized. Having a family was what made living so worthwhile. He hoped for as long as he lived that he'd have his family around like his parents did.

That night after everyone was in their rooms, he and Autumn sat on the couch and read. He'd finally gotten around to hanging the television and was glad now he'd gotten one to fit the room. The kids were enjoying it more than either of them were, however.

"Oh, by the way, Joey. I'm pregnant." She turned the page on the book she was reading as if she'd not just told him the best news. "I don't know how we're going to manage this, but I will admit to you I'm having a great time."

Taking cues from her, he flipped the paper to the next page before speaking. "By then, we should be pretty good at getting car seats in and out of the van, as well as changing diapers. Dad is really good at it." Autumn looked up at him from her book. "Are you happy, love? Do you feel all right?"

"Terrified, if you want to know the truth. I do feel good, however." He watched her. "I don't want anyone to know just yet. I mean, I never want to feel like I did before either, but I'd like to hold onto this for just a little while longer. If you don't mind."

Joey moved to pick her up in his arms and held her. The two of them, sitting there on the couch, made it a bit tight. Using just enough of his magic to make it wider and softer for the two of them, he wrapped them both up in one of the many lap blankets that had been in this house when they moved in.

"My grandma has always had a way with looking at just bits of the future. Not a lot of detail, but enough that she could work things around so the outcome was better if that was needed. Today when I was talking to her, she told me she'd seen the two of us, not your face but my mate, living in this house with our children. Then she told me what else was in her second site that day." Autumn asked him if it was bad. "No. She told me this house would forever hold more than just the two of us. That someday our children would need to come home with their families because of a death. There would be celebrations too, larger than anything we've seen so far. Grandma also told me you and I will have a great many more children coming through our lives that we will cherish and love like no other child has been."

"Children of our hearts and bodies, I hope." He nodded. "I'm glad for that. Being alone for as long as we were, the two of us, we need this. I've never, in all my life, thought I'd love being a mother and an aunt. That having someone around me, other than you, would bring such joy to me." He told her what he'd thought of today when out shopping for cars. "Exactly. That's it. We will make sure our family never has to wonder if we love them. I want to be able to hug all of them when they need it, and I need it. Yes, Joey. Being with you is the best thing that has ever happened to me. I don't think for as long as we live, there will be anything that tops my love for you and this family."

Joey and Autumn made love that night. It was soft, gentle. And when they came several times, it was not just explosive as it usually was, but warming. Gentle. Even too much at times. Holding her afterwards, he knew when she'd fallen asleep and got up. Ending up in the yard where he usually did, he reached out to the earth to find and fix what he could.

Joey? He paused in his work to listen again for the voice that had contacted him. *My name is Toby. Toby Townhouse. Aurora told me I could find you here if I were patient. I'm in need of your help. Please?*

He didn't immediately tell Toby he'd help but reached out to Aurora. She told him the man was telling him the truth, and he could help him.

Toby isn't human, not that I think you would care, but he is a faerie. He would like to talk to you about your daughter. He met her today. Robin is his mate.

Joey wasn't sure how he felt about that but contacted Toby. *Aurora told me you're Robin's mate. She is only seventeen and plans to go to college. I know you've met her, but I'd like you to take your time in presenting yourself to her. She hasn't had much of an opportunity to be who she wishes to be.* Toby said he understood that. *If you hurt her, Toby, there will be no place you can hide that you won't be found.*

You'll kill me. He told him it wouldn't be just him, but all of the Whitfield tigers. *Yes, I thought you'd say that. I won't hurt her. I swear it. I am a secondary faerie, which means I'm ancient. Almost as old as the earth. If she would allow me to, I'd like to begin slowly, as you said, and introduce her to some of the magic I have for her.*

For as much as he wanted to tell the faerie no, he knew now that he'd found her, there would be nothing he could do. Having Toby promise him that he'd take it very slow with her made the man happy. He wondered how Robin was going to take this and laughed.

You are on your own, Toby. But as I said, you harm her, and you'll be a dead faerie. I'm stronger than anything on this earth, including you. Do you understand me?

Toby did. When he came out of the wooded area near where he was sitting, two things struck Joey. Toby wasn't just a faerie, but a grand one. A royalty as close to Aurora as he could be without being her child. Also, Toby was tall, like he was. When he bowed to him, Joey bowed back with his head.

Thank you, your lordship. I shall see to her in the morning. Joey nodded. *I have the means to care for her in the way you have. If you would allow it, my lord, I will see to it that she's able to get her education as well as anything she would ever want.*

Joey told him again it would be up to Robin. He could only hope she was more like her aunt than her mother. Otherwise, it was going to be a hell of a ride for the two of them. As he went into the house, he got into bed with his wife. Tomorrow. Tomorrow his daughter would meet her mate. Joey was glad he was going to be around for it.

Before You Go...

HELP AN AUTHOR

write a review

THANK YOU!

Share your voice and help guide other readers to these wonderful books. Even if it's only a line or two, your reviews help readers discover the author's books so they can continue creating stories that you'll love. Log in to your favorite retailer and leave a review. Thank you.

AWARD WINNING, BESTSELLING AUTHOR

Kathi Barton, a winner of the Pinnacle Book Achievement award as well as a best-selling author on Amazon and All Romance books, lives in Nashport, Ohio, with her husband, Paul. When not creating new worlds and romance, Kathi and her husband enjoy camping and going to auctions. She can also be seen at county fairs with her husband, who is an artist and potter.

Her muse, a cross between Jimmy Stewart and Hugh Jackman, brings her stories to life for her readers in a way that has them coming back time and again for more. Her favorite genre is paranormal romance, with a great deal of spice. You can visit Kathi on line and drop her an email if you'd like. She loves hearing from her fans. aaronskiss@gmail.com.

Follow Kathi on her blog: http://kathisbartonauthor. blogspot.com/